I'M
FRANK
JOHNSON

H.E.ROFFEY

To my sons, Dorian and Carl, who are mostly oblivious of their huge contribution to my life and my writing.

I thank my wife, Sonja, for her many rereads and corrections. Without her support, patience and love, this book could not have been written.

H E Roffey, January 2021.

CONTENTS

Preface 9

One 10
Two 11
Three 14
Four 17
Five 21
Six 23
Seven 29
Eight 34
Nine 36
Ten 44
Eleven 46
Twelve 52
Thirteen 55
Fourteen 58
Fifteen 61
Sixteen 64
Seventeen 67
Eighteen 70
Nineteen 73
Twenty 77
Twenty One 80
Twenty Two 83
Twenty Three 87

Twenty Four 89
Twenty Five 97
Twenty Six 100
Twenty Seven 104
Twenty Eight 107
Twenty Nine 115
Thirty 118
Thirty One 121
Thirty Two 124
Thirty Three 128
Thirty Four 132

Author's Note 136
About the Author 138
Also by Harold Roffey 139

PREFACE

The second in a series of novels exploring the actions of various characters as they face pertinent social and moral issues.

ONE

We'd agreed to meet at the café at twelve thirty. By one fifteen, I'd finished my snack and was too anxious to concentrate on the Sunday paper. It had gone two o'clock by the time I left and had walked to the lake. Strangely enough, my anxiety had waned. I put it down to the intervening hour or so that forced me to reflect on my role in her life and, although I felt I'd relinquished my responsibility by simply leaving, I also felt free of her. I knew she wouldn't be able to phone me if she'd become involved in another arrangement, and I certainly wasn't going to put her at risk by phoning. I also think I faced the truth of my motivation for being there: I wanted this extremely attractive, young woman to need me. But now I felt elated by our disentanglement and free after a long time of internal conflict, so I decided to walk home instead of using public transport. I took a deep breath and pushed my shoulders back as though beginning a marathon rather than my estimated three-hour walk. By the time I reached the outer ring road of Regent's Park, I was well into my stride and impatient to cross, as I waited for a break in the traffic, not knowing that Zuzanna was dead.

TWO

Everyone knew everybody else's business on our small estate in West London where I grew up. Youngsters developed according to their desires and strengths and, to some extent, what others thought of them. Snippets of information – good, bad or indifferent – would find their way through gossip, whispers or forthright comments. Only later did I learn that the older generation was aware of stories, false or otherwise, about whom you were according to their prejudices and experiences. I shouldn't have been surprised then, when aged nineteen, I felt secure enough to share my secret with my long-standing girlfriend, Lidia, also nineteen. She told me her version of the same story, as given to her by her mum. It made me tingle with shock. Even now, whenever it inadvertently crosses my mind, I have a knee-jerk reaction. However, she accepted the story from me as a token of my trust, and I considered it to be a further element that bonded us together.

When I was eight, I learnt from my mum and my stepdad that my real dad died when I was two and a half. I tell this story in different ways depending on who's listening, but when I told

Lidia, I found myself reaching deep into my soul for every detail, including my treatment for acute anxiety when I was eleven.

People said I couldn't have remembered my real dad, but I knew that wasn't true. I couldn't tell you what he looked like, but I definitely know it was him who'd made me laugh when I was picked up in a particular way.

I remember an event involving a man who could only have been my dad.

I didn't expect to cry while telling Lidia, but although I did, I wanted to tell her everything. It felt as though I'd collected all the fragments of the story and was assembling it accurately so that I could store it away and forget it.

I remembered hearing a woman shouting, I told her. There was also a screeching sound and the smell and taste you get while the dentist is drilling. I definitely heard loud voices and felt my pushchair shaking. I know I was crying loudly while a woman, with a big face, was pulling me out of my pushchair.

I was also shaking while telling Lidia. I unashamedly looked into her face and saw my fear reflected in it, but I couldn't stop and I didn't want to.

The woman with the big face was holding me tight against her and was jogging me up and down. I can remember having no-one I knew near me. It was a feeling I can't describe. I think I was terrified, but that's just to put a label on it. Then I remember seeing Mum at home. I don't know how I got there. She looked different. My gran seemed to be with me after that. I can't remember seeing Mum again, but she was somewhere about.

Years later, I was told that my father had tripped near

the edge of a railway platform and had fallen on to the track and died. I used to ponder this possibility. I'd study the edges of platforms for things on which to trip whenever I was at a station. I was aware that I couldn't ask my mother about that event then, or even now come to that, without her becoming upset, consequently the story is incomplete. However, when I was eleven, I asked if my father had been with someone when he'd tripped. I remember Mum looking at my stepdad instead of answering, and he looking back at her.

'You were too young at the time. You were in a pushchair,' I remember Mum saying.

I didn't mean to alarm Lidia. In fact, I thought I'd be able to describe my non-committal reaction to Mum's answer without emotion. However, I shocked myself and frightened Lidia by screaming as I'd probably done aged two. I put my face in my hands and leaned on the table while Lidia nervously rubbed my back until I'd recovered.

'And that's why I started seeing a shrink,' I said glibly a minute or so later, in the hope of bringing the story to a comfortable end.

'Did your mum tell you she was in a mental hospital for months after it happened?'

She could tell by my frozen expression that I'd not heard that before. I was also tingling with thoughts about how other people viewed my family.

Lidia took my hand.

'That's what my mum says.'

I didn't answer.

THREE

I can't tell you about Lidia without first mentioning Frances, our eldest daughter, now twenty-seven. It was during the very early stage of Frances's gestation that our family was kick-started and two years after I'd fallen in love with Lidia.

I'd felt very distraught when Lidia dropped me for some guy she'd met at work. Looking back, I shouldn't have been surprised. We were both twenty-one, and I'd assumed too early in our relationship that we'd be together forever, in spite of me warning her of my "mental fragility" as I called it. Our parents often met up and, when I heard that Lidia was unhappy and not seeing anyone, I dropped by Lidia's parents' house one morning, in the hope of catching her before I went on contract with my firm for a few days.

Joe, Lidia's dad, hesitated before ushering me into the kitchen to join him for a cup of tea.

'I do hope she's going to be OK,' said Lidia's mother, Elsie, before coming through the doorway and catching sight of me. She looked worried and, instead of greeting me with her normal bearlike hug, she put her hand to her mouth. Joe glanced at me and, without permission, I shot upstairs to Lidia's room and found her packing a case. Her face crumpled, as she backed away with the flat of her hand held towards me.

'Go away!' she shouted.

'I'm not going anywhere until you confirm what I suspect.'

Without my questioning, she blurted it all out. She'd steeled herself to have an abortion.

'I was stupid,' she sobbed. 'It had no meaning. I want my life back as it was.'

'As it was when?'

'As it was with you.'

'Are you absolutely sure?'

'Yes!' she screamed, holding her face in both hands and letting herself slide down the wall until she was crouching.

'I want to hear you say it,' I shouted above her sobbing.

'I want you back. I'm so sorry.'

I can't remember exactly when her mother came into the room and saw Lidia on the floor, with me standing over her.

'Come,' I heard her mother say, 'it's time to go, love.'

In that second, I saw Lidia with a child as one complete person, and I wanted her.

'She's not going, she's coming with me.'

I ignored her old man's, 'Are you sure?'

I felt like hitting him for doubting me. Elsie and Joe started talking in weeks and months about things to be done as though they were in charge, while Lidia was treated as a problem and I was helping them out. I'd had enough.

'You want me and you've got me. Get your things while I make some calls.'

15

Lidia's smile said it all. She was up and out of the room in a flash. Half an hour later, my van was ready for the first of many trips to my small flat.

Lidia and I had fish and chips at a local café that evening. I felt invigorated, and she looked radiant. Seven months later, she insisted on the name "Frances".

'Without you, she wouldn't be here, and when she's old enough, I'm going to tell her everything.'

Five months after that, Lidia's mum and my mum took turns in rocking the buggy to keep Frances quiet while the registrar married us.

FOUR

I'm Frank's wife, Lidia. I want to squeeze in at this point because no two people have the same view of an event and, besides, Frank wouldn't be able to express my emotions as I would like.

I thought I was destined for greater things when I was young. An office job in a new glass building in London as a receptionist was to be my first step. I felt success in my bones. I was going places. Although Frank warned me of his "mental fragility", as he called it, it never showed itself. Besides being good-looking, he was loyal, down to earth and had realistic ambitions. Compared with him, I was out with the fairies. I saw part of my progress as throwing caution to the wind, not realising how naïve I was, or how self-centred the young men, who greeted me each morning, really were.

I did my utmost to appear aloof and sophisticated, by replying to Charles that I'd let him know by lunchtime about joining him for a drink after work. Drinks after work led to a dinner a week later. I'm not going into detail here, but I felt I could step off the "down to earth and personal ambitions" and go for the "wealth and good times" offered by Charles. Looking back, I don't know that he actually offered anything of the sort. I slept with him after our third dinner date. "Slept" – what a ridiculous euphemism. I thought that having sex with Charles had cemented our relationship in place, so I could tell Frank it was all over between him and me. Yes, I did tell Frank. He turned away without a word, and although I remained resolute, I felt less confident as I watched him get into his car.

The following Monday, Charles greeted me with a compliment which was typical of the other young go-getters. I didn't expect a loving comment or anything like that, but I did anticipate some subtle acknowledgement of our relationship. However, there was nothing further that day, or the next, or the day after that. I felt so humiliated and used that, on the following Monday when he passed my reception desk, I asked him if he abused all women or was it just me. I remember, to this day, how he stopped for a second and, with a silly grin, glanced at the other men at the desk who were collecting their messages.

He walked away, but he'd only gone about four steps when I stood and shouted, 'Don't walk away from me when I'm bloody well talking to you!' Then an older man came to my side of the desk, took my arm and asked me to calm down. I shook myself free of him, grabbed my bag from the shelf and my coat from the stand.

The last thing I heard, as I walked away from that beautiful desk in that beautiful building, was, 'Charles, see me in my office immediately.'

I was devastated when I found I was pregnant. I confided in my mum, and I suddenly felt I was on an equal footing with her, as she shared confidences with me. The following day,

I confirmed my decision to have an abortion and, without any hesitation, she told my dad, who was equally supportive and handled all the arrangements while I carried on with my new job as an administrative assistant at a nearby Toyota franchise.

On the day of my appointment for the abortion, I heard Frank talking with my mum and dad downstairs and, seconds later, he was in my room without knocking. I shouted at him to go away, but he kept coming towards me. I thought he was going to hit me, as he looked so wild. I don't know if Mum or Dad told him, but he seemed to know I was going to have an abortion.

'Yes. I'm pregnant!' I screamed. 'And I've got to go.'

I can't remember everything, but I desperately wanted him to hold me. There were tears running down his face, and when I said I wanted my life back as it was, he wanted me to spell it out. My legs folded and I slid down the wall after I screamed "yes" when he asked me if I wanted him back.

I couldn't believe my ears when he said, 'You've got me, and you're coming with me now.' My mum came into the room. I think she thought Frank had hit me. I certainly felt I deserved it.

Having an abortion didn't worry me as long as my thoughts didn't dwell on the baby. I couldn't believe it when I realised Frank wanted me, child and all. I sat at the kitchen table feeling uplifted. I laughed and cried at the same time while Frank was businesslike, making phone calls and riding roughshod over everything Mum and Dad suggested.

That was the first time I witnessed Frank's inner strength. He had warned me off him early in our relationship and even said he didn't think he had a grip on life and he'd be a burden.

I know his father's suicide lives with him and his forays into therapy during his life have focused on his lack of self-worth, but I think he shows strength by admitting his weaknesses. However, knowing his mum, I wouldn't be surprised if it's genetic. She's been in and out of a mental hospital for years.

FIVE

I've been occasionally envious of Frances's bond with Lidia as she's got older, but I've since realised Frances has been concerned about me, even when she was young. It's made me wonder if it stemmed from us being bonded by our love for each other without being blood relatives.

I remember her excitement when she was eleven and Lidia and I were expecting Becky. We were thinking about names when Frances twigged that "Frank" was an abbreviation and that there was something strange about our names sounding similar. Lidia used the opportunity to talk to Frances about the reason and, Frances being Frances, questioned both of us over the following two hours or so. She then gave us each a hug and said she was going to tell her friend, Claire. Lidia and I knew Frances well enough to know she was unlikely to dwell on questions in the privacy of her room when she'd always been given comprehensive answers to satisfy her mature curiosity. Nevertheless, it wasn't the outcome we'd expected, but she had always been confident with a "take it or leave it" attitude, and this knowledge about herself, seemed to give her an extra uniqueness which she valued. That evening, she followed me to my office and questioned me about Lidia, after giving Lidia the third degree earlier. Lidia and I had anticipated these questions and had agreed to be completely honest with her. As a result, she seemed to savour the information and was excited to have been given it. I also felt she'd grown an inch that day and had taken on the mantle of an older person, but I'm sure that was my imagination playing tricks.

Looking back, I've relived that wonderful feeling of being hugged extra tight.

SIX

Lidia and Frances had gone to the cinema while I took advantage of the warm spring evening by walking from our house to Putney Bridge. I stopped, as always, to feel the excitement of the River Thames streaming either side of one of the bridge's buttresses as it seemed to speed through the incoming tide like the bow of a ship.

Normally, I'd return home from there, but knowing my other two daughters were also out, I walked on. Cafés were closed, and I didn't feel like imposing on a restaurant, when all I wanted was a drink.

At fifty-two, you'd think I wouldn't need courage to go into a pub but you'd be wrong. Sometimes being six two and weighing eighty-five kilograms is the shell in which I hide. I pushed the door open and got a whiff of spilt beer and instantly felt alone. The pub's spacious, dark-brown interior and stained-glass windows expressed solid permanence in the face of modern surroundings and a group of its regulars, who were cajoling a large, middle-aged barmaid, appeared to be part of the pub's stand against change.

'After you,' I said while standing aside for a tall woman who took advantage of the throng at the bar's counter to push in front of me.

Her somewhat aggressive glance at my response was automatic and protective, she told me later, but for that moment, she carried on looking at me until I looked down hoping she'd place her order and move on. I was still looking down when I heard a barman ask her what she wanted.

'Please serve someone else. We've not made up our minds,' I heard her say. She was still looking at me when I looked up. In fact, she grinned and the remnants of her frown evaporated when I smiled back. She then laughed which caused me to smile more. Then her frown slowly returned.

'I'm sorry I elbowed my way in. I feel really bad about it.'

'It's really OK.'

'It's not OK, but thanks for saying it.'

I smiled and nodded towards the bar for her to resume her position, but she carried on looking at me.

She raised her eyebrows and held out her hand.

'My name is Zuzanna.'

She breathed out and allowed her shoulders to relax, as I took her hand.

'I'm Francis Johnson… Frank.'

I followed Zuzanna's eyes towards a group of overzealous, young men and women standing in loose formation around a couple of tall pedestal tables.

'I'm with them.'

'Looks like a celebration.'

'It's Friday, that's all. Come and join us, not everyone knows each other. One more'll make no difference.'

'Thanks, but I won't.'

'Then let me buy you a drink to make up for my bad behaviour. What would you like?'

She tried to persuade me to have something alcoholic, but I justified my pint of soda and lemonade by briefly telling her about my walk. Then I reached for my wallet.

'No. Put that away. This is definitely on me. Grab that table by the wall before someone else takes it.'

I rearranged two worn, red leather chairs around a small table while Zuzanna distributed drinks among the people in her group. A couple of heads turned towards me. One man caught my eye and acknowledged me by holding his glass up in the manner of saying cheers.

'Shouldn't you be with them?'

She plonked herself down and clinked her glass against mine.

'They're too wrapped up in their own stories to miss me. And, quite frankly, I'm glad to be out of it.'

I glanced in the direction of their conspicuous laughs and was reminded of similar feelings at gatherings after work when I was a company executive.

'Their banter is not only boring, but their testosterone is generating enough aggression to stage a military attack. Most of us are in sales, so perhaps we should be forgiven if our competitiveness spills over into leisure time. Anyway, tomorrow will be Saturday and I'll be myself again.'

'And what is yourself?'

Her smile faded, as her frown returned, while she slowly and deliberately put her gin and tonic down and continued to look at it for a few seconds with her head to one side. *Rather like a blackbird listening for worms on a lawn*, I thought. She then raised her head and searched my face with her large, dark eyes.

'We've only just met, and you're asking a very personal

25

question.'

'What could be better? I'm sure we could both gain something from the conversation, say goodbye and never see each other again.'

'OK,' she smiled. 'Tell me something about you.'

'Fair enough. I'm old enough to be your father, unless you're older than you look, but you'll possibly find the life of a house decorator boring.'

'You have a company then?' she interjected while glancing at my light, summer jacket and Paul Smith shirt.

'Yes. I'm its only employee, unless you count my wife, who occasionally helps with the books.'

'You don't look a bit like a house painter.'

'Decorator! And how many house decorators do you know?'

'None. And seeing that you're setting boundaries, I'm thirty.'

I enjoyed telling Zuzanna about Emma, Becky, Frances and Lidia. It gave me a chance to assess my immediate life and, just as I thought I was beginning to bore her, she prompted me with further questions.

'Wasn't it a bit arrogant to name your daughter Frances? Sounds the same as yours.'

'It was Lidia's choice… She wouldn't budge,' I quickly added after a short pause.

'Why?'

I laughed as always when the subject comes up, because it has never failed to make me feel proud of Lidia's stubbornness about the naming of Frances.

'That's definitely a story for another time. Now it's your turn.'

'Perhaps we'll not see each other again, so what's the harm?' she said with an upwards intonation on the word "perhaps". 'But I still want to know the answer.'

'Zuzanna is a Polish name,' she said. Then she spelled it out. 'My parents came here when I was fourteen and poured every penny they had into my brother's and my education, but he died in a car accident ten years ago when he was eighteen.'

She started talking in cold, factual terms but, within a minute or so, she became quite animated and sat forward in her chair and studied her glass. The more she talked about her many friends, the lonelier I felt she was. She stopped, looked directly at me and leaned closer.

'Are you interested in football?'

'Highlights sometimes. Why do you ask?'

'Essono ring a bell?'

'Afraid not.'

'Jordache Essono's my boyfriend. But I see you're not impressed.'

'I'm neutral.'

'Are we in complete confidence here?'

'Yes, but I don't want you to wake up tomorrow regretting something you've told me.'

'Jord is a bit of a celebrity, and the press love to get their teeth into anything. I would like to have married him, but he wouldn't commit. I think he regards his football career to be more important. I've since seen a side of him which makes me less sure, and a couple of guys from work have warned me off him.'

'You no longer want to marry him?'

'I don't know. I've reflected on my parents' unhappy life,

and it's made me think again.'

Zuzanna took another sip of her gin and tonic and told me how she and her mother were more financially secure since her father died while working on a building site, and the insurance had paid out.

'When I said they poured every penny into our education, that wasn't quite true. My mother worked hard and did the pouring. My father drank a lot. Mum stopped being abused, and I no longer felt responsible for her, so it wasn't as bad as it sounds. You've now heard more than my best friends, and I'm stopping before I describe how I was potty-trained.'

'And how were you potty-trained?'

She laughed and held out her empty glass.

'I need another drink after that,' she said before glancing at the pub's clock. 'Oh my God! Look at the time! I must go. Jord will be furious.'

She rummaged through her bag before handing me a couple of business cards and a pen.

'Please write your name and number on the back.'

I had an ominous feeling while writing my name on the card and very nearly didn't give it back. In haste, she snatched it from me, read my name and number aloud, swept her long, dark hair to one side and kissed my cheek.

'Thanks for listening, Frank.'

SEVEN

I retained images of Zuzanna's smooth-featured face, large, dark eyes and elegant figure as I walked back home from the pub. However, in spite of my natural inquisitiveness about her predicament, I had no intention of making contact with her.

I glanced at her business card when I got home, "Zuzanna Wadzinski – Senior Accounts Manager" and dropped it into my office shredder where the sudden noise punctuated the end of my thoughts about her.

I didn't mention Zuzanna to Lidia. Wished I had now, but then I was more interested in what Lidia and Frances had to say.

Four weeks later while I was on a ladder carefully painting a window transom, Zuzanna phoned.

'See you at the Red Lion. Thursday at six or phone me back after eight tonight.' The phone went dead.

'Bugger!' I muttered as the next brush stroke touched the glass.

I felt extremely guilty as I walked the half mile or so towards the Red Lion from the empty house where I'd been working. I hadn't phoned Zuzanna and was half hoping she wouldn't be there.

'Lost in thought?' I heard her say. 'I've been trying to catch you up for the last fifty yards.'

I turned in time to receive a kiss on my cheek.

'Glad I caught you. Let's go to a café I know instead. How long have you got?'

'No more than an hour.'

She slipped her arm in mine and guided me away from the Red Lion. 'That sounds like a consultation,' she laughed.

'Who for, you or me?' She laughed again, as she opened the door to the café. I went to the counter to get the drinks while she found a table away from the window.

'And was Jord furious?' I asked as I put her coffee down.

'Do you remember everything people tell you?'

I didn't answer. She rested her elbow on the table, held her chin in the palm of one hand with her fingers spread over her lips, while her eyes flicked from me to the table and back a few times.

'He sulked.'

'And after the sulk?'

Instead of answering, she slowly stirred her coffee so as not to disturb the heart-shaped chocolate surface.

'That's an appropriate metaphor.'

She stopped stirring and carefully removed the spoon.

'What metaphor?'

'Trying to maintain appearances and the taste at the same time.'

'I don't understand.'

'Isn't that what you're trying to do with your relationship

with Jord? You want all the benefits of being with him while preserving your independence.'

She looked up as her mouth formed a smile, belying the sadness in her eyes.

'OK, clever clogs, tell me how a house painter...'

'Decorator!'

'How a house *painter* knows I need to sort myself out?'

'You told me.'

'What did I say?'

'You said you had wanted Jord to marry you, but you've since seen a side of him that's given you doubts, and you've been warned off him by people you appear to respect. And, of course, the fear you expressed when you thought he would be furious with you for being late.'

'Wow! Where do I go from here?'

I looked from her eyes to my hands, thought for a moment, looked up to reply and saw her jaw quivering. I opened a packet of tissues and handed her one. She wiped her eyes.

'I'm sorry.'

'There's no need to be sorry. I think your chat with me at the pub was a cry for help. You saw me as a father figure and that's why you wanted to meet me again.'

'Now I'm feeling silly.'

'You feel it, but you're not.'

'Any advice?'

'Talk to people who have your interests at heart, your mother for a start.'

'I can't. She told me to break my relationship with Jord ages ago. She said guys like him regard women like me as trophies, which led to an argument, which I found insulting.

31

And besides, she's a racist and Jord is Cameroonian.'

'So what! She's your mother and going back to her will probably boost her respect for you.'

'You don't know my mother.'

'Friends?'

'I'm afraid something will get back to Jord. He seems to have systematically rejected my friends, and I've never been one for having a best friend.'

'Then find yourself a good counsellor.'

'Are you abandoning me?'

'I'm giving you the best advice I can.'

'I think I'm beginning to learn why a house painter recommends a counsellor. I'm guessing, but I think something happened to you. What was it?'

I felt unexpectedly exposed to this young woman whom I hardly knew. I studied the table, to collect my thoughts, before describing my feeling of not deserving the position of director of a large building company a few years back.

'I kept aiming for higher and higher quality rather than an economic balance and eventually I felt incompetent. My heart wasn't in the money side of the business, and I was voted off the board with a substantial payout. I didn't understand it at the time. As far as I was concerned, I was a failure and then I had a breakdown. It took two years to understand I'd been a square peg in a round hole. I went back to something I knew and enjoyed, and now I'm my own boss. I guess that's what they call a blessing in disguise, because I couldn't be happier.'

Zuzanna had been studying me while I spoke, and although I'd felt emotional, I'd not lost my composure. I was then taken aback when she reached for my hand and squeezed it.

'But I'm not ill.'

'Neither was I when I joined the board, and that's why I recommend you see a counsellor while you're well and able to rationalise your feelings. Why try and solve it by yourself? Treat yourself to some dedicated time with a professional.'

'I am treating myself. I'm talking with you,' she grinned.

'I'm not a counsellor,' I said, 'and I can only give you limited advice.'

'I probably wouldn't take advice anyway,' she laughed.

She looked relieved, and I felt apprehensive while promising a further meeting but then, having decided to tell Lidia about Zuzanna, I felt uplifted. Colours appeared brighter and the air felt clearer in the early evening sunlight.

EIGHT

I still felt uplifted, as I hopped on to my driveway from my van. Everything looked sharp-edged and clear, and I couldn't wait to give Lidia a hug. She's not demonstrative; not prudish exactly, more prim, as though keeping herself prepared for some future event. I've failed to get her to be more spontaneous but, nevertheless, I love her for who she is and I accept being scolded on the odd occasion.

Lidia smiled, as I turned her small frame away from the kitchen countertop, on which she was preparing dinner, and then she pulled away, as I squeezed my hands across her back to see if her bra would come undone.

'Emma and Becky are in the front room and Frances will be here soon. You'll have to wait till later. You can get Frances's room ready. She's staying the night while her flatmate's away.'

I slipped my hand through the waistband of her skirt and squeezed her bottom.

'Now you can tidy me up,' she said holding out her food-covered hands.

I've not had sex with anyone other than Lidia. I've not

confessed that before. Don't ask me what held me back from such adventures. It wasn't religiosity, and it certainly wasn't lack of desire. There'd been enough spent semen in showers when I was young to endorse my imaginative skills about film stars, sisters of friends and a school teacher who only had to look at me to make me go red all over. Sex and love came packaged with Lidia, and I felt that any unbundling would diminish both.

That night, our antics did seek new boundaries and she somehow ditched the primness I described earlier. I watched her sitting over me with her medium-length, greying hair hanging forward and framing her small face. I was enraptured by the sight of her lightweight figure moving up and down and back and forth against the dimness of our bedroom. And as she closed her eyes, with her hands on my chest, and threw her head back making a noise as if in pain, I felt I could devour her. Then she fell on top of me and gasped.

'I'm sure Frances could hear us through the wall,' I whispered, as Lidia leaned across me to retrieve a box of tissues.

'Good!' she replied kissing my arm. 'Goodnight... Sleep tight.'

NINE

Zuzanna had turned the tables on me, at our last meeting, by correctly guessing I'd recommended she see a counsellor because I'd found counselling beneficial myself. I toyed with the idea of phoning her to ask if she'd made any significant decisions. However, I knew she had aroused other feelings within me, which scared and excited me, so I didn't phone.

Time spent thinking of Zuzanna had dwindled to just about zero after two months and, if by chance I did think of her, my heart wouldn't jump as it had done. I had hoped that my sex life with Lidia had been permanently spiced up and she'd loosened up a bit, but no, she went back to being restrained, as though letting herself go, as she'd done that night, had made her more vulnerable.

The hair on the back of my neck rose with the sound of Zuzanna's voice on my phone.

'I know you take Fridays off. May we meet at eleven this Friday?'

I think she was aware of my hesitation.

'Please make it. I'm hoping to claim another hour with you.'

She laughed as I reached her table.

'Do I have an hour?'

I took out my phone and exaggeratedly set the alarm.

'Ready, steady, go.'

She came to my side of the table and kissed my cheek.

'I couldn't wait to get here. I've taken the rest of the day off whether you're available or not.'

I immediately regretted my casual use of the phrase; 'unfortunately I'm not,' for fear of its possible misinterpretation and its hint of a future time. *I'm getting paranoid*, I thought, and then a shiver went through me, as I thought of my past paranoia.

'Oh well, I'll just have to make do.'

Then I wished I'd said, '*Let's make the most of the hour*' but it came out as 'Let's make the most of the time we have together,' making me feel like I'd stood on a landmine. She then put her hand on top of mine confirming that I possibly had.

'I've decided to get out. I've been living with Jord for over a year in a penthouse overlooking the Thames. He's spent a fortune on me but, in truth, I think he regards it as compensation for him being away training or playing.'

She became increasingly animated as she talked about her life with Jord: the daily delivery of flowers, the unlimited credit on her bank card, the extravagant parties and expensive food and drink, the maid, the on-call service, the dress designers and the rest until she refocused on her surroundings. It felt like she'd returned from a hallucinatory trip and had just managed to land back in the same place. I'd become bored and wondered how someone, as bright as she appeared to be, could drown in something so shallow. *Was she trying to impress me, or was she assessing the benefits of staying with him, or what?* I was at sea and let her talk until her repetitive chat left her empty.

'Knock, knock. Is there anybody in there?' she asked tilting her head to one side and looking at me.

'You're hoping the pros outweigh the cons. If you're talking to me in the hope of a revelation, you're wasting my time and yours. I don't mind being a sounding board, but I can't help you decide. I think you've made up your mind but lack the courage to leave him. If that's true, then stop beating about the bush.'

Her lips drooped at their edges, then she sat upright and blinked.

'That was really harsh.' Then she mumbled, more to herself than to me, 'Is getting out the only answer?'

'I'll repeat the only piece of advice I've given you: talk to a professional if you really can't talk to your mum. Talk to Jord and get him to go with you.'

'What? You mean like a marriage counsellor?' She scoffed as though I'd suggested major surgery.

'Why not?'

'I know what Jord would say to that.'

I didn't comment.

'You've bloody well abandoned me.'

Yes, I thought. *I am abandoning you, along with something of me.*

'Well?' she questioned after a few seconds.

'You're attractive and intelligent, but you're not my daughter. You have the tools to handle your life, and your choices are now exposed. You need courage and that's something I know nothing about. I hope I've helped.'

My little speech probably benefited me as much as her. However, she reached across the table and took my hand.

'I don't want you to think of me as a daughter,' she said looking suddenly serious.

I felt as if she'd removed the barriers to her mind and body for me. I put my hand on hers, let it go and stood up. Zuzanna rose from her chair, leaned forward to kiss my lips, as I turned my head to kiss her cheek.

'In that case, twice more, I'm Polish, remember.'

My little speech – well, that's what it sounded like – cauterised any feelings I had for Zuzanna, and I hoped it had done the same for her about me. Consequently, I was surprised to see Zuzanna's number on my phone as it rang, two weeks later, while I was cleaning the van.

I could hear her desperate voice, 'Can you hear me? Can you hear me?' long before I managed to put things down and juggle the phone to my ear.

'I can now.'

'Please, please meet me. Friday at four, same place.'

The phone went dead.

I dwelled on the anxiety in Zuzanna's voice and became infected by it during the two days that led up to that Friday.

Contrary to my expectations of finding Zuzanna in a distressed state, she was smiling and already seated when I entered the café.

She stood and carefully kissed my left cheek.

'How's the house painting business?'

'Show me what's happened.'

She pushed her hair from one side of her face and kept

her eyes to the other while I assessed the age and impact of the bruising. By the time I'd asked when, why and how, tears were streaming down her face.

'I'm sorry,' she said.

'There's nothing to be sorry about.'

'The day before I phoned you, he pushed me and I hit the corner of the door.'

The bruise was too evenly spread to come from the corner of anything, and I guessed she'd been hit by a fist.

'If you tell me lies, I'll leave,' I said handing her a table napkin. She started to sob.

'I'm sorry.'

'For lying or crying?'

'Please don't bully me. I can't take it.'

'Go to the loo, and I'll get you another coffee.'

I'd initially steeled myself to be jovial regardless of how I'd find her. I had even toyed with the idea of inviting her home to meet Lidia, and for her to spend the evening with us, in the hope she'd be able to look at her situation more rationally. However, my imagination got the better of me and I pictured her using my house as a refuge and disrupting my family.

'He lost his temper and hit me.'

I waited for her to elaborate, but she resorted to repeating the many ways Jord was making her reliant on him.

'We've been through this before. Did you do anything about seeing a counsellor?'

She sighed, let her shoulders sag and bit her bottom lip, giving me a glimpse of the child she once was when given a problem she couldn't solve.

'I looked online when I got back from seeing you. The

following day, Jord wanted to know why I'd been searching for a shrink. He said shrinks were for mad people. He didn't want to hear any more about it, and I wasn't to do it again. He hardly ever uses a computer, so I guess one of his guys was spying on me. There's always someone in the apartment.'

'How did you get here?'

'Jack was the only one in the apartment. He's a nice guy, always attentive and never off his phone. I waved at him from the door as I left. He seemed a bit alarmed and got up as if to say something. I got out of the lift in the car park, quickly started my car and drove to a parking lot not far from here and caught a taxi.'

'Social services will help and may even offer you immediate protection.'

'Isn't that a bit over the top?'

Looking back, I wish I'd been more forceful with my advice, but she answered me with less concern than I'd anticipated, and I began to think that, apart from the evidence of violence, she might have exaggerated her story to create a drama as an alternative to boredom.

'I suggest you let social services be the judge and, even if you don't take up anything they have to offer, I'm sure you'll feel better after talking to them, and besides, it's confidential.'

'I'm sure Jord'll find out.'

She dismissed my idea of using a public phone, and I didn't offer her mine.

'And the senior account management job?'

Zuzanna told me how Jord belittled her by saying how pathetic her salary was compared with his and that her work problems were petty. She then went on to tell me how he'd started turning up at the pub where she'd meet her workmates on a Friday and how he unsuccessfully tried to use his celebrity status to muscle in, and when that didn't go well, he took it out on her when they got home for undermining him in front of them. She said she couldn't prove it, but she thought he was the reason she lost her job, making her totally dependent on him.

'And then, as if all was forgiven, he threw a huge surprise party for me with guests from all over. I'd seen some on TV or in magazines, but I'd not met them before.

'When the party was over, he accused me of flirting with someone I couldn't even recall. I then accused him of being pathetic. The next thing I remember was waking up with a doctor sitting on the side of our bed while Jord explained how I'd been drunk and had fallen on the marble floor.'

In spite of hearing about her abuse, and the many other reasons for leaving Jord, I felt frustrated by her inability to focus on the possibility of leaving him.

'That's the best I can do,' I said moving my seat back. She picked up her bag and walked into the street with me. I returned her kiss on my cheek with a kiss in the air near her ear while she held me tight.

'I've thought about you every day since we first met, Frank. Is this really the closest you're going to get to loving me?'

I thought my nerves had been exposed, as she snuggled up against me. It took a moment or two before I felt calm enough to release her. I then held her at arm's length, leaned forward, kissed her cheek and watched her eyes fill with tears.

'I feel so sad that you don't have more time, Frank.'

I was so afraid of the sound of my voice and the words I might have used that I simply squeezed her hand and turned away.

The area was livening up and cars were now parked tight against the kerb of the narrow street. A large, dark-skinned man got out of a four-by-four, apologised for blocking my way and closed its door. I looked back after crossing the road and saw the same man enter the café.

Zuzanna phoned the following Thursday, but I got no response to my repeated hellos. My phone rang again half an hour later.

'Please meet me on Sunday at 12:30 at the café in Regent's Park.'

'I'm sorry, Zuzanna, but I won't.'

She gasped for breath as Emma had done when she fell off her bike and broke her arm.

'I'll stay on the line. Take your time. I won't hang up.'

'It's the… ohn…, it's the… ohn…, it's the… oh…'

'Breathe deeply and take your time.'

'It's the on…ly day I can make,' she said between sharp intakes of breath. 'Please…'

I could hear voices in the background before the call was terminated.

I have no truck with people who believe in fate, but the hair on the back of my neck rose when, after searching my mind for excuses to meet Zuzanna, Lidia apologetically said she wanted to take Emma and Becky shopping for clothes on that day, knowing I wouldn't want to tag along.

'Please don't worry about me. If it's not raining, I'll probably go for a really good walk. I need the exercise.'

TEN

Swans, geese and many species of duck waddled along the edge of the boating lake in Regent's Park in the hope of picking up titbits from eager children trading their sandwiches and the like for the thrill of watching each bird greedily fight for every morsel. The air was still, and the low sun shone sharply through the leafless mid-November trees. It was the sort of scene that might be captured in the mind but rarely by a camera.

I half expected Zuzanna to be at the café in spite of being fifteen minutes earlier than her anxious cry for 12:30. By one fifteen, I'd let my imagination run away with me as to why she would be late. However, I managed to calm down over the following half an hour while thinking rationally about the many possible reasons for her not turning up or phoning. By two o'clock, I felt buoyed up by feeling free of her and decided to walk home instead of using public transport. I did, however, carry a sense of loss which seemed to gain weight the longer I walked.

Not being able to keep things from Lidia became evident soon after returning home.

'There's definitely something on your mind.'

There was no point in hiding it. I made up some cock and bull story about feeling exhausted after my long walk.

'Go and shower now. The girls will give you a fashion parade after dinner – and you have to say you approve.'

As I became immersed in the chit-chat of the evening, I realised how close I'd been to jeopardising the trust of my family and undermining the mainstay of my support, Lidia. I had a huge sense of relief knowing I could put Zuzanna behind me and knuckle down to work, convinced that my guilt would soon fade and that I would never again hurt myself by breaking Lidia's trust in me.

ELEVEN

I heard the doorbell, but I knew Lidia was aware of me being buried in my evening's administration work and would soon answer it. A minute or so later, she came into my office.

'There are two police officers to see you. I don't know what they want. They wouldn't tell me.'

And that's how I met young, small and neat Detective Sergeant Mary Cummings and a large constable whose name I didn't catch and didn't think relevant.

'Tea or coffee?' asked Lidia.

'No thanks,' said Cummings. 'We just want to ask your husband a few questions.'

'I'll leave you to it. Shout if you need me.'

It sounded a bit odd to me when Cummings stated; 'You're Frank Johnson?' as if framing a question.

'Yes, I am. What can I do for you?'

'We're hoping you can help us. Where were you on the ninth of November last year?'

'I'll need to get my diary. I'll be back in a sec.'

'It was a Sunday,' I heard her say, as I turned to go to my office.

What's that got to do with anything? I thought before the

significance made me tingle all over.

I'm one of those people who are easily frightened by authority, any authority. I've only got to see a brown envelope on the mat and I imagine Inland Revenue printed on it before I've picked it up. It may only tell me my tax code but it's too late, the feeling's been aroused and I won't be able to shake it off for an hour or so. A routine road stop by traffic police can easily make me depressed for the rest of the day. I've never faced up to the reasons for this, even while I was getting myself back into shape with therapy after my breakdown. I know it's anxiety and, strange as it may seem, I get comfort from knowing that life doesn't go on forever. *I know I should revisit this issue with further therapy.*

Examining my work planner in the privacy of my office was futile, but going through the motions helped settle me and seemed to put my story into context and confirm its authenticity. The small square depicting that Sunday was blank, apart from the pencilled cross, which now appeared ominous as it nestled in one corner like a spider. I had no premonition then of its future significance, but when it sunk in that it was symbolic of Zuzanna's intended meeting with me, I tingled all over. I sensed something serious had happened. I took a few deep breaths to overcome feelings of nausea, waited a minute or so to gather my senses, and braced myself for bad news.

'You were right,' I said holding out my diary as a token of my absolution. 'It was a Sunday and there are no entries.'

'Where were you on that day?'

I think I coloured up slightly. I could certainly feel the vein in my neck pulsing while she and what's-his-name waited for an answer.

'My wife went shopping with my daughters, and I went to Regent's Park for the day. I know that because of a note on the previous Thursday.'

'What time did you leave the house?' asked Cummings.

'Soon after Lidia, so it must have been about 10:30. Perhaps if I knew what you were looking for, I'd be able to help.'

I felt more confident having said that.

'We're investigating a murder and looking for anyone who may be able to help us,' said Cummings.

As I recalled Zuzanna's desperate last words, my throat dried and my tinnitus took on a high pitch. I thought my involuntary intake of breath and raised eyebrows were enough evidence to indicate I was not simply a bystander. Cummings and what's-his-name looked deadpan and their neutral stance told me nothing. *Did she take revenge and kill Jord?* I thought. *Or has she been murdered?* I felt desperate for an answer.

I was conscious of the passing seconds and tears slowly filled my eyes.

'That's awful,' I said taking a packet of tissues from my pocket. 'Where did it happen? Who was it?'

'You seem upset,' said Cummings.

'Don't worry about me. I sometimes find it difficult to look at the news on TV without tears and occasionally I buy the paper and daren't read it.'

All that was true and hours of therapy had not resolved it. In fact, my counsellor had said, 'Let it happen. You'll find people will accept it and you'll feel better.'

'And a murder is so sad, regardless of who it is.'

'At this stage, we're eliminating people from our enquiry,'

said Cummings.

I must have been as thick as two short planks because the word "alibi" still hadn't dawned on me.

'I'm sorry I can't help you. The only fighting I saw were swans having a go at each other over a slice of bread.'

'Did you ever come into contact with a woman by the name of Sue..., Sue Wadzinski?' asked the constable looking at his notes.

I'd not known the origin of the saying "blood running cold", but I felt my left arm go numb. I concentrated on the unfamiliar "Sue" and what's-his-name's mispronunciation of "Wadzinski" in an effort to separate me from the person they were talking about.

'Afraid not,' I replied.

'If you think of anything at all, please ring me on this number,' said Cummings handing me a card.

I sat in the lounge for a minute or so after seeing them out. Then my right heel jumped when I realised I'd not asked where they'd got my name from.

'What did they want?' asked Lidia.

'They were looking for help with a murder case and wanted to know where I was on that Sunday I went to Regent's Park.'

'Why you?'

'I've no idea. They weren't forthcoming. They're probably asking a whole range of people.'

'That's horrible... anyway, dinner'll be ready in ten minutes.'

'Can it wait a bit? I don't know why, but their questioning has given me a headache. I'd like to lie down for a while.'

Lidia was accustomed to my fear of authority, just as she was aware of my vulnerability. Perhaps she carried some of my emotional baggage for me, but her calm attitude contradicted that.

'It's a little early for dinner anyway. I'll call everyone in half an hour.'

I lay on the bed imagining Zuzanna being murdered. I considered phoning Cummings, but the thought of having to share the information with Lidia was unthinkable.

'*I can understand the first time you met her, but what about the next and the next and the one after that?*' she would have asked, all the while shrinking further and further from me. '*And why didn't you tell me?*' would have been her absolute, final and appropriate question for which I'd shored myself up with lies to avoid.

Gripped by unbearable anguish, I buried my face in a pillow and sobbed. Twenty minutes later, I got up and washed myself from head to foot, in the shower, as if using the flannel as a piece of sandpaper.

This will all go away, I told myself as I dropped Cummings' card into the kitchen bin on my way to the dining table.

'Who were those people?' asked Becky.

'There's been an accident and someone got hurt and the police are looking for help,' interjected Lidia.

'I couldn't help them,' I added.

'Was it near here?' asked Emma.

Lidia looked at me for help.

'It was about two months ago when I went to Regent's Park,' I replied.

'How was school, Emma?' asked Lidia. 'What did Mrs Williams think of your history essay?'

Emma's smile said more than words and her inner pleasure overshadowed her concern for the victim of the accident. Becky stopped frowning and, within seconds, any thoughts the girls had about the accident soon vanished.

TWELVE

From the day of the visit by the police I concentrated on my work, but tiredness from fitful sleep, and thoughts of Zuzanna, caused silly errors that became amplified into imagined catastrophes at four in the morning, and the perfection I was aiming for eluded me.

At two one morning, I imagined telling Lidia the whole story. I lay awake for the next couple of hours imagining her saying, 'Tell the police everything. Hurry before the evidence evaporates. I'm sure it was the boyfriend. She told you he was violent. You said you saw the bruising. She told you she was frightened of him and the person who killed her is probably still out there.' However, I consoled myself with thoughts of competent men and women having got the culprit, and I eventually fell asleep.

I was sure Lidia knew I'd been preoccupied since the police visit, but knowing me as well as she does, I think she chose to let its impact on me gently fade. If that was the case, then she was correct. Rational thinking about Zuzanna's murder gradually supplanted my vivid imagination, and I became less tormented by my denial of her to the police. However, three months later, while Becky and Emma were out, I opened the front door to Cummings and what's-his-name.

'Do you know a man by the name of Jack Travner?' asked Cummings.

'Never heard of him. Why?'

'Your name was on a list he gave us,' said what's-his-name. 'He says he knows you.'

'I'd remember a name like that. He's not been a client of mine. Why would I know him? What did he say? Is this something to do with the murder of that woman?'

'It is,' replied what's-his-name.

I felt secure with the truth, as I sat in an armchair watching them perch on the edge of the settee opposite.

'The last time we spoke, you said that you left home at about ten thirty to go to Regent's Park and you returned at about six that evening. Please tell us what you did in those seven and a half hours.'

'I'll be back in a moment,' I said getting up. 'I need to go to the toilet.' I quietly went to the stairs to avoid Lidia seeing me from the kitchen. One look of concern, or possibly a question from her, would have reduced me to a wreck. I sat on the toilet with my head between my knees to get the blood pulsing.

'Sorry about that,' I said as I went back into the room.

The pair hadn't moved, but Cummings looked genuinely concerned as she asked if I was OK.

'Yes, sorry. I mentioned before that I get attacks like that. I get nervous in front of officialdom. Always have done. Like a kid in class going red. I've not grown out of it. Sorry.'

I suddenly felt much better with that off my chest.

Hooray for therapy, I thought.

I described the day as it happened and how I needed time to myself to read and relax; a place in the open air, get some walking exercise and eat and drink when I wanted.

'And then I walked home.'

'You walked from Regent's Park to here?' questioned Cummings.

'Yes.'

'How long did that take?'

'Under three hours, even with my stop to look at the McLaren showroom in Park Lane.'

I searched my mind for proof of my day's outing before they asked. I remembered joking with the woman at the café who served me hot chocolate and a Danish pastry. That receipt was long gone, but I told Cummings anyway.

'Ah, yes,' I added, 'I bought the papers at the local shop at about eleven and said hello to Ibrahim as usual.'

'What about later that day, say between two and six? Did you notice anything or come across something or somebody that could substantiate your whereabouts?'

Why didn't they simply say, 'Have you got a believable alibi?' and leave it at that? I described everything I could remember.

'I'd been lost in my thoughts most of the time and had wanted to walk where there was as much green space as possible. I remember the river being low, but I couldn't tell you which way the tide was running along the Chelsea Embankment.'

'You've got my card,' said Cummings. 'If you think of anything at all, please ring me or Constable Edwards.'

'May I have another card?'

THIRTEEN

'They wanted to know where I'd been between two and six on that Sunday.'

'Why?' asked Lidia.

'I think they're doing their best to remove superfluous information from their enquiry into that murder.'

I felt uncomfortable when Lidia started asking me questions but, as I said, Lidia has seen me through the worst and is the only person who uses the word "breakdown" with true feelings of support without taking me back to those lost months. Her antennae seem finely tuned to my whatever-it-is, and she homes in to my vibrations within microseconds. I, in turn, recognise that she wants to reach out and help me.

'Come sit,' she said taking my hand.

I know she also regards me as a sort of hero. I'm occasionally conscious of her watching me in the morning, from the kitchen window, loading the van in preparation for battle. I return with trophy enough to maintain our family in more than reasonable order. And so, when our little camp here in Putney appears to be under attack, we are equally hero and heroine facing the world.

I obeyed, and we sat together on the settee where, only a

few minutes earlier, Cummings and Edwards had sat.

'Can you think of anything? Anything that will stop them questioning you?'

'The police focused on the four hours between two and six,' I said.

Lidia knew I often went for long walks, although three hours was unusual. She also knew that, had she not gone shopping with the girls that day, she would probably have been with me and, as a result, I think she felt a tinge of guilt.

'I think they're scraping the bottom of the barrel,' said Lidia. 'They've probably only got circumstantial evidence and now they're questioning half of Putney because someone said they'd seen you out walking. I wouldn't be surprised if the whole neighbourhood is being questioned. Try and forget about it. You've helped them all you can, and you'll probably find the case will be solved without you.'

She pecked my cheek before going into the kitchen, but I couldn't forget her using the word "probably".

My work was no longer the perfect quality I habitually strived for, and I had horrific nightmares that lingered long enough to dovetail into daytime imagination. There was nothing for my brain to chew on, and I was becoming neurotic. The overwhelming guilt of being dishonest with Lidia was leaking into my very soul and making me question everything. *Did I really walk home from Regent's Park? What else did I do? I gave up on Zuzanna and she died. I'm failing to communicate with Lidia, Emma and Rebecca. I rely on Frances's visits, and I don't pop in to see her any more.* I felt my sanity slipping away.

I sensed Lidia's relief when I said I'd like to go to Regent's Park and retrace every step.

'If it helps you shake free of this thing, whatever it is, then you must do it. Do you want me to come with you?'

'And the girls?' I questioned.

'They'll enjoy the house to themselves. Don't worry about them.'

FOURTEEN

I felt heartened by being together to solve "our" problem as Lidia called it. I'd not seen it that way till then. The more I talked as we walked, the lighter and more animated Lidia became. We almost forgot the reason for going to Regent's Park, as we chatted over lunch. We even fed the ducks from the bridge as I'd done.

'Did you really walk all the way home from here?'

Normally I'd have thought nothing of a question like that, but I took it seriously. It questioned the foundation of our trip, as though we'd become actors in a charade.

Lidia's face grew ashen when I said, 'Of course I bloody well did. I wouldn't have said it otherwise.'

We left in silence. Fortunately, the tension between us was broken by our mutual interest in the ring-necked parakeets taking off from a plane tree in Hyde Park.

'What about possible roadworks and building alterations at the time?' asked Lidia.

I couldn't remember any, and when she asked what McLaren cars were in the window on that day, I knew we were clutching at straws.

'It's a pity you always pay cash, as credit card statements

would have given you proof.'

'Yes. You're right.'

I draw cash frequently because I don't like to carry much, but then it dawned on me that perhaps I'd drawn cash from an ATM that day. I never keep the receipts and rarely request one. I stopped to think.

'What's up?' asked Lidia.

'I can't remember drawing cash that day, but perhaps I did. I know I didn't queue for a machine, but I can't remember checking if I had enough cash for the day as I usually do.'

'Surely that's something you'd remember?'

'Sorry,' I replied, wounded by what I perceived as criticism.

I then started to panic, as I felt her support slipping away. I stood in the street close to tears, unable to see, and started to shake. I sensed Lidia's alarm. I could hear her voice, but her words were muffled and far away. Suddenly, her face was in focus a few inches from mine. She spoke concisely and clearly.

'OK. We're going to stand still for a minute, and then we're getting a taxi.'

'What did I do on the Saturday before that Sunday?' I shouted. 'I need to look at my diary... I need to look at my diary...'

'We'll do that when we get home,' she said into my ear while holding me tight against her.

I remember sobbing loudly in the street and in the taxi. Everything else was a blur until I felt Lidia lift my head from her lap. I felt drunk as we made our way to the door, but that's all I remembered until Lidia helped me sit up and take some tablets. I knew nothing of the phone call to Frances or the emergency services. Apparently, I ate something and took myself off to bed.

Ah yes, I also remembered my relief at not having to face the girls as I entered the house.

FIFTEEN

'Mum told us what happened, Dad. Are you OK?' asked Becky at breakfast the following morning.

Instead of answering, I shoved my chair back, got up and went to her and kissed the top of her head. I then kissed the top of Emma's head.

'Yes. Things got a bit on top of me yesterday, but I'm OK now.'

I joined the rest of the conversation as best I could, but I felt thwarted by the woolliness caused by my medication. My mind drifted to the time of my breakdown, and I wondered how the children had experienced it then, aged five, seven and eighteen. I'd felt ashamed at the time and saw myself as a failure; no longer the hero, no longer the protector of the family.

After breakfast, I felt well enough to get myself back on track without taking another tablet. Lidia had made an excuse to stay home for the day and, once the front door closed leaving the two of us, we calmly cleared things away. Half an hour later, and against Lidia's advice, I went upstairs to my office.

'Don't worry,' I said, 'I won't be long. I'll probably go

back to bed.'

I'd resigned myself to thinking there was no cash withdrawal on that Sunday and, having accepted it, I put the bank file away, took out a black marker pen and wrote a list on an A3 sheet of paper and pinned it to my work board.

Stay calm
Keep anxiety under control
Be completely honest
Substantiate where you were on that Sunday
I'm innocent
Who is Jack Travner?

I returned to bed and fell asleep within minutes. I awoke just after midday in time to have a snack with Lidia.

'I'm going out,' I said.

I persuaded her not to go with me and, like a child, I promised (not that I blamed her) to be back by four o'clock. I took a bus to a point where it would have taken me a couple of hours to walk home along the same route as I'd taken on that Sunday.

Although my bank statement had no entries for that date, I needed to finish the route, hoping it would jog my memory and settle the matter about cashpoints along the way. However, by the time I got home, I'd convinced myself I'd drawn from at least three of them and discovered nothing new.

I could sense Lidia's eyes on me throughout the evening, while Emma and Becky carried on with their chatter.

'Don't even think about Jack Travner,' said Lidia once the girls had left the room. 'It was a good idea to write things down though.'

Besides imparting her thoughts, Lidia had subtly indicated she'd been in my office.

'I felt better just by writing it. Did I miss anything out?'

'No, I don't think so, but try and relax a bit and don't get yourself worked up about justifying your whereabouts. I was a bit concerned about you stating your innocence. You know you are. Perhaps you should add something about taking your medication more regularly.'

I thought about Lidia's comments, especially about me being innocent. In the end, I left it on the list because it seemed to give me comfort. Thereafter, every time I went into my office and looked at that A3 sheet pinned to the board, I felt my stomach muscles relax. However, I have to confess, I felt anxious about being totally honest if I was questioned further, but I knew it was necessary for my own sanity.

My resolve to adhere to my written instructions was tested when, three weeks later, I answered my phone to Cummings.

'I'll be home by three thirty. Could we make it then?' I asked, knowing the girls would be out until six or so.

SIXTEEN

'I think I should be with you,' said Lidia. 'I'll come home early.'

'If you'd prefer it, but I'm sure I'll be OK.'

'I'll think about it. Love you.'

Tough it out regardless of the questions or who's there, I thought. 'Please support me, Lidia,' I heard myself whisper.

It didn't take long for Cummings to get to the nub of the issue.

'You said you hadn't heard of a woman by the name of Sue Wadzinski?'

'I know a Zuzanna,' I replied without hesitation.

I was surprised that neither Cummings nor Edwards showed any emotion. *They'd probably heard many excuses about minor name mispronunciations before*, I thought, and because I wanted to redeem myself in their eyes, I immediately launched into the hows, whens and whys about my meetings with Zuzanna without further questions.

'If you thought of her as a daughter, why didn't you become upset when you suspected we were possibly investigating her murder?'

'As I said, I'd distanced myself from her long before

that Sunday, and I was numbed by the thought of her being murdered. I'd given her all the advice I could and I'd shut her out of my mind. I also believed I had no information that could possibly help you.'

I dared not look at Lidia while I was being questioned.

'Did she actually say Jordache hit her?' asked Edwards.

'Yes. At first she said he pushed her and she hit her face on the door.'

'Did you believe her?'

'No. I told her I would leave the café if she told me lies. She then told me he'd hit her.'

Edwards took notes, while I recounted as much detail of what Zuzanna had told me. The more I spoke, the more I realised that my imagined voice of Lidia had been correct. *There'd been things the police could have followed up on.* I began to feel diminished, negligent and relieved that neither Cummings nor Edwards alluded to it.

'Can you tell us about Jack Travner?' asked Cummings.

'I don't know anybody by that name. How does he fit in this jigsaw?'

'He's also helping us,' replied Edwards. 'Did you manage to remember anything further about your Sunday afternoon walk home from Regent's Park?'

Reluctant indulgence or boredom showed on the faces of both Cummings and Edwards, as I described my failure to reveal anything while retracing my steps with Lidia. I knew its only relevance was a pathetic display of my apparent innocence and it counted for nothing towards their enquiry. However, they both interrupted with questions about me requiring a taxi and a doctor near the end of the walk.

I couldn't tell if Cummings and Edwards were assessing

my mental stability or not, but their questioning stopped soon after. Lidia, by then, was crying.

SEVENTEEN

I followed Lidia along the hall to the kitchen where she turned on me like a lioness rejecting its mate, her metaphorical claws fully displayed. I stopped dead. She gave me a dismissive look and continued walking. She then opened a cupboard door and took out a packet of rice.

'Don't say a word. Do – not – say – one – word. Dinner will be ready by the time the girls get here.'

I touched her arm but she withdrew, spilling some of the rice. She ignored it, put both hands flat on the countertop, letting the packet fall on its side and stood with her head hanging forward. Her anger was palpable and her hurt crippling. Her tears fell among the rice grains. I felt frozen and impotent.

'What can I do?'

'Do absolutely nothing.'

She swept the spilt rice off the countertop into a saucepan and added more from the packet without measuring it.

I'm ashamed to say that I slunk off to my office and made it shipshape in an attempt to, at least, tidy up that part of my life. Halfway through, both girls came into my office. Emma's lips were down at the corners, her eyes were gleaming and she was near to tears. Becky was not smiling and seemed to be tight-jawed as if ready for a fight.

'What's up with Mum?' Becky asked.

'Your mum's annoyed with me.'

I was about to tell them more when Lidia shouted to us for dinner with a tone that commanded unusual obedience. Both girls hurried to their rooms to drop their bags.

'You will tell me all about it?' questioned Becky without smiling.

We, Lidia and I, loved our chats with the girls at dinner, and the loss of intimacy and the fragmentation of our common bond that evening reverberated long and deep, as Lidia hurt herself and the rest of us with her curt responses. Becky and Emma finished their dinner quickly in unfamiliar silence, excused themselves from the table and disappeared to their rooms.

I hoped to break the impasse as we cleared the table, but Lidia replied with dismissive responses to my comments and apologies. She left me to finish clearing up and went to the lounge and switched on the television.

Feeling bereft, guilty and ill, I took two of the previously prescribed tablets instead of one and told Lidia I was going to bed. I kissed her cheek, but she did not respond. I was also anxious to talk with Becky and Emma. I couldn't bear the thought of them feeling cut off from Lidia and me, and I'm not ashamed to admit that I felt I needed them. I knocked on Becky's door. It opened immediately and without any prompting, Emma, who looked as if she'd been crying, put her arms around me while Becky, again looking serious, hung about until I hugged her. I sat down on the bed next to Emma while Becky dragged her chair closer.

'What have you done, Dad?' asked Becky.

'Your mum is upset because I withheld information from her when I shouldn't have. I haven't actually done anything wrong so you needn't fret. Your mum and I will sort things out shortly. A young woman I met has died, and the police want as much information as possible from everybody so that they can find out what happened to her.'

'Was that the accident Mum told us about?' asked Emma.

'What didn't you tell Mum?' asked Becky.

'I didn't tell Mum about meeting her. It didn't seem important enough to tell anyone, but the woman wanted to meet me again because she thought I could help her with some personal problems. I met her a couple of times after that and, rather than explain the whole thing to your mother, I'd decided to tell the woman I wouldn't meet her again.'

I tried to read Becky's face, as she studied mine from less than a metre away. I thought that Emma, being only thirteen, had a fertile imagination equal to her elder sister but less focused on the machinations of human relationships. However, it was Emma who broke the silence.

'Was she pretty?' she asked, giving me a jolt.

'She was and only slightly older than Frances.'

'And did you?' asked Becky.

'Did I what?' I replied feeling defensive after Emma's question.

'Help her.'

'I wish I knew the answer to that.'

I was unsettled under their scrutiny and wanted to close the conversation before my medication took hold.

'Enough for now. Ask as many questions as you like tomorrow. I'm feeling tired even if you're not.'

EIGHTEEN

I believed that Lidia's continued dismissive attitude towards me would diminish of its own accord if I didn't allude to Zuzanna or anything else relating to the case. However, she seemed to build a barrier to reinforce her new stance, leaving me devastated.

I enjoyed my work and so I buried myself in every aspect of it – the communications with clients and suppliers, my constant striving for perfection and efficiency and the management of the business, right down to the minute details of my office. It became my refuge and I was no longer distracted or made silly errors. The sheet of paper remained pinned to my planning board, and although the words on it had become my mantra, I felt they'd lost their power to keep me stable, but the last thing I wanted was to go back on medication.

I was delighted to see Frances when she came into my office one evening. In truth, I was quite emotional when she hugged me and then plonked herself down in a chair.

'Come on, Dad. I want to know all about it.'

She used my own tactics on me: she waited for an answer without interrupting or adding words to influence my reply.

'How much do you know?'

'Mum told me about the session with the police the other day.'

'And?'

'She's upset because she learned things then instead of being told by you.'

'I've explained my reasons to your mother, but it doesn't seem to make any difference.'

'She's hurt, but she'll get over it, Dad. I'm more worried about you isolating yourself. Emma and Becky know something's pulling their nest apart, and they'll soon be thinking you've had an affair, if they haven't jumped to that conclusion already.'

'The girls seem OK-ish with me, but I can see they go out of their way to please their mum. I wish Becky's spontaneous smile would return, but I don't comment. And Emma has become a bit clingy. I'm sure it will all come right in the end.'

'You might have to spell it out to Becky about not having had an affair. She told me you said you've done nothing wrong, but that might not be sufficient, Dad.'

'Well, I haven't.'

'Even if you had, you're here with us now, and Mum's feeling vulnerable. It might be a good idea to clear the air by telling the whole story to all of us at the same time.'

Frances was correct of course, and she'd already done the groundwork. Lidia reluctantly agreed to have all of us together for *my confessional* as she sarcastically called it. I found the process painful. It wasn't cathartic; in fact, it amplified my feelings of guilt and reinforced the gap between Lidia and myself. Perhaps she felt less special by being one of four women being treated equally. Frances, on the other hand, kept close and made an effort to bridge the gap. I wanted Lidia back as she had been with all my heart. *A highly supportive daughter is still a daughter*, I thought.

I'd defensively ring-fenced my work activities. All my contacts were kept abreast of my work, schedules became tighter, without sacrificing quality, and materials were perfectly labelled and stored. The office, workshop and van were kept immaculate and suppliers were nurtured. You could say it was a squeaky-clean operation. I extended my working week to include Fridays and Saturday mornings.

I'd become tougher, more resilient and possibly more self-sufficient, and seeing Cummings and Edwards at the door a few weeks later hardly fazed me. Lidia asked if she should join us, but when I told her there was nothing I could add, she left me with them.

NINETEEN

'Sorry to call on you again,' said Edwards.

'You say you've not heard of Jack Travner. Is that correct?' asked Cummings.

'I've no idea who he is.'

Cummings took a couple of pictures from an envelope, turned one to face me and handed it over.

'Do you recognise this man?'

The dark-skinned man's face and upper body filled the whole picture. His high cheekbones and thin face accentuated his charming smile, and his bald head seemed unusual for his young appearance. He was wearing a light sports jacket, a brightly patterned tie against a dark blue shirt. He seemed confident, as he stared directly at the camera. The background was blank, as though prepared for the picture. I looked away and put my head on one side and closed my eyes while I searched my mind for clues.

'There's something familiar about the man, but I can't place him. I do remember Zuzanna mentioning a nice young guy who was often in the apartment. I think she said his name was Jack.'

'His name is Jack Travner. He said you killed Miss

Wadzinski.'

Being the sort of person that went red in class when the teacher wanted to know who had done whatever it was, and picturing myself as a child when I was first questioned by Cummings, I momentarily saw Cummings as a "Miss Cummings". Not that I had ever had a Miss Cummings at school, but it took a second or so to recover.

'He says he left you with her and when he came back, he found you standing over her body. Do you still confirm you've never met him?'

'Absolutely!'

The lounge door flew open and Frances, wearing a plum-coloured raincoat and a storm hat, filled the doorway.

'I'm sorry! This is not on,' she said. 'Nobody should speak to my dad on his own.'

'But…' I started to say.

'Sorry, Dad,' she said before turning on the officers. 'I know my dad better than anybody. He'll go out of his way to give you any information you want and make himself vulnerable in the process. This is not on and what's more, you were told how vulnerable he was the last time you were here.'

I watched Cummings' calm face, as she justified her presence by saying they were not making an accusation but gathering information.

'How do you know how your bloody evidence gathering is interpreted in the minds of others?'

Edwards was about to say something when Frances continued.

'That's right. You don't bloody well know.'

Cummings didn't move or falter.

'I'm sorry to have caused you or your father distress,

Ms. Johnson. I'm Detective Sergeant Cummings and this is Constable Edwards.'

Frances calmed down during the ensuing silence and removed her coat.

'In the interest of efficiency, we'd like to continue. I believe we are nearly finished.'

'If you must. Dad's got nothing to hide.'

'What were you about to say regarding this picture?' asked Edwards.

'I've never met him. And as for him saying he left her with me... that's ridiculous!'

'And this one?' asked Cummings handing me another picture of the same man holding a phone.

'I've described the café, the black four-by-four and how I glimpsed the person who closed its door, but I couldn't swear it was the same man.'

'I think that's all we need. You've been most helpful. Have a good evening,' said Cummings, as they both got up. Frances walked with them to the door, and I heard them saying their goodbyes.

'Did Mum just leave you with those two?' she asked, as she walked back into the room.

'Don't be hard on your mother. She's had a lot to put up with and, besides, I told her I'd handle it myself.'

'Please, Dad, make sure you have someone with you. If you have to testify for whatever reason, you don't want some smart-arse lawyer nitpicking between every word. The less said the better.'

I was beginning to feel like a child in the face of Frances's forcefulness. I also felt defenceless and physically nauseous from guilt as though I'd been accused.

That was the first intimation I had of all my perceived, accumulated guilt being bundled together. I could feel my grasp on my innocence slipping away. I wanted everything to end without caring how. I'd been at that twilight zone between sanity and something else before, but it still didn't give me the tools to deal with it.

TWENTY

I was part way through telling Lidia about the pictures of Jack Travner and his accusations when, with a look I found difficult to read, she said, 'And did you know him?'

I felt cold with shock, and I had a sudden ringing in my ears. I searched her demeanour for some emotion, but she seemed oblivious of her remark or its impact on me, and continued reading some business journal.

I couldn't respond and went to my office feeling empty. I sat and looked at my work planners in the hope of seeking a diversion to stop me from slipping further into the void, but everything looked superficial and futile. I needed fresh air. I got up, put my coat on, silently closed the front door with my key, entered the cold, dark evening and made my way to Putney Bridge.

I once again looked at the bulging, weed-covered buttress of the bridge, as it appeared to speed through the incoming, muddy water. I knew I was vulnerable without my medication but sane enough to understand the misery I'd cause if I jumped. I remembered feeling tortured and alone but very little after that.

I knew where I was the moment I heard the indistinguishable chattering of muffled voices and felt my body being moved about. I started to mouth something, knew it was unintelligible and gave up. I felt too sleepy to try again, and I didn't have the wherewithal to open my eyes.

'Hello, Dad... Dad... It's me, Frances.'

'Leave him to sleep. You lot go home, and I'll stay,' I heard Lidia say, as I felt my hand being stroked.

I heard Becky's voice. 'He's moving.'

'Hi,' I whispered without opening my eyes.

'Are you OK?' asked Emma.

I moved my fingers, but my eyelids were too heavy.

The sound of a curtain being pulled along rails and a woman cheerfully saying good morning woke me. I pushed myself to a sitting position and squinted about me.

'Your wife will be back in a few minutes. I'm Dr. Balakrishnan... Janet.'

'Morning,' I croaked.

'Do you remember what happened?'

I told her about looking into the river and described what I could.

'We've given you a sedative, and you've been in hospital since eleven last night,' she said referring to a file.

'How did I get here?'

She flicked over a few pages and silently read before giving me a summary.

'You were brought here in a police car by two officers. You were wearing a vest, trousers, shoes and socks, and you had a blanket over you that came from the police car. Don't worry if you can't remember.'

I flinched, as I recalled screaming, tearing off my coat, jacket and shirt and throwing them over the wall of the bridge. I remembered talking to a policeman in a car and thinking how kind he was, but I didn't remember getting in or out of the car.

'Apparently,' she continued, reading from the notes, 'a middle-aged couple saw you and phoned the police. They stayed with you until the police arrived.'

'How did my family find me?'

'Your wife phoned just past midnight to see if you'd been admitted. You fitted her description, and she came here at 00:35. Is there anything else you'd like to ask me?'

I suddenly felt exhausted.

'No, thank you. I'm OK.'

'The nurse will be here shortly with some tablets. Get some rest, and I'll see you tomorrow morning.'

I think I was asleep before the curtain was closed. I woke when I felt my hand being stroked. Without looking, I knew it was Lidia.

TWENTY ONE

The taxi came to take me home from the hospital within ten minutes of my call. It was either that or be fetched like a pet from the vet with no independence.

'I told you to call me,' Lidia said when she opened the front door.

I kissed her cheek.

'I think you should lie down for a while. Sleep in Frances's old room where you won't be disturbed, and don't go fiddling in your office.'

I interpreted her one-sided stream of advice as mistrust of my ability to fend for myself. I didn't argue. Immediately after catching up on things with Lidia over tea and biscuits, I went upstairs to my office, gathered keys together to make a new set, opened my mail, initiated new bank cards and searched for anything that could put the last few days behind me.

An hour later, and with a look of disapproval, Lidia helped me reschedule my work so that I could be up and running as soon as possible.

'There's a lot of it going about,' clients had told Lidia when she'd phoned them to excuse me from my work commitments.

'It'll look ridiculous if you turn up after six days when I told them it would be at least ten.'

I looked at Lidia's serious profile. Eye sparkle missing, bright clothes in the cupboard and hair held back with a clip. I'd not seen that before, and I hated it. My God, I missed the real Lidia.

I did sleep in the afternoon and woke up as I'd planned, two hours prior to dinner. I scrubbed myself pink and felt better having chased the soapsuds down the shower drain with a hot-water spray.

'Thanks but no,' replied Lidia to my offer of help. 'Besides, you look as though you're dressed for an evening out, and you might get something on you.'

I hung about feeling ineffective.

'Can I get you a drink?' I asked, as I prepared the table for five.

'Only water for me.'

Emma and Becky came home together and hugged me.

'Are you better now, Dad?' asked Becky.

'You're not going back are you?' asked Emma.

'Enough!' said Lidia before I could answer. 'Stop questioning your dad. Dinner will be ready as soon as Frances gets here. She's only got an hour.'

Ignoring Lidia, the girls waited for an answer.

'I'm fine,' I said holding each in turn until they laughed and struggled to get free before retreating to their rooms.

I was still faffing around in the kitchen when I heard Frances in the hallway.

'Hello sibbies!' she shouted to the girls from the bottom of the stairs.

Becky and Emma's feet hit the stair treads as one continuous ripple until they reached the hall. I was torn between wanting to join the three of them and get a dose of Frances's enthusiasm, or being with Lidia as a confirmation of my loyalty. I knew it was a pathetic gesture, and I sensed Lidia was aware of it, but I resigned myself to it not knowing how to break the pattern without exposing myself further. I may as well have not bothered because, although Frances was sensitive to the family's dynamics, she was never going to let it get in the way. She came into the kitchen, her stature and forceful good nature filling it, and with a quick 'Hello Mum,' she gave me a hug, then stood back, held my arms and looked into my eyes.

'You'll do!' she said before hugging Lidia.

Thank God for Frances, I thought.

TWENTY TWO

I was almost relieved when I opened the door to Edwards and Cummings a few days after their last visit. Conscious of their disregard for Frances's words about surprise visits, I accepted their apologies and invited them into the lounge.

'Have you ever been to Beaconsfield?' asked Edwards.

'Yes. It was a few years ago. Why do you ask?

'We're curious,' said Cummings. 'You've not asked us where or how Miss Wadzinski was murdered.'

My head instantly filled with the very worst of my nightmares of Zuzanna's murder. *I felt I could see her disfigured face and her one remaining eye looking at me. Blood: wet, glistening and streaming from her hair and over large, gravel stones between railway sleepers.* I could not speak, and I couldn't face knowing the truth. And now these people, who might have the answer, were taunting me. I thought of shouting *I don't want to know,* or even putting my hands over my ears like a child if they started to tell me. I could hear the noise of a train. I could hear a child screaming.

Lidia described what followed. She said she heard me screaming and ran from the kitchen to see what was happening. She pulled Edwards aside, as he knelt beside me. Apparently, I had my hands over my face, and I was crying. Cummings told Lidia I'd suddenly looked about the room, put my hands to my face and fell forward on to the floor screaming. I remembered keeping my hands against my face while Lidia was trying to prise them off. I could see her mouth moving, but I couldn't hear anything.

'Are you OK?' I asked her. 'Is anybody else hurt?'

I wondered if I'd been injured, as I was helped into a chair. But then, Cummings and Edwards came into focus, while I grappled with what had happened. It was rather like a dream one tries to grasp soon after waking, only to find it as elusive as clutching at air.

'What did you do? What did you say?' asked Lidia.

Cummings and Edwards looked at each other as if a slight pause may prompt the other into replying.

'No accusations, just simple questions,' replied Cummings.

'All questions are simple,' Lidia shot back at them.

'Perhaps it would be better to postpone it for now,' said Cummings.

'I'm sorry,' I said. 'I had a vision of us being in a terrible accident, but I'm over it now and I'm feeling OK. I'd rather we finished. I don't want this thing dragging on.'

'I'll stay then,' said Lidia while lowering herself on to the arm of my chair.

Edwards looked at Cummings who was looking at Lidia.

'Go on then,' prompted Lidia impatiently.

'You asked about my lack of curiosity about Zuzanna's murder,' I said.

Cummings, who had resumed her position opposite me,

raised her eyelids revealing a frown that increased her age by five years. Edwards had a similar expression while glancing at her as if seeking a cue.

'Would you like to add something?' asked Cummings.

'I can't explain my reaction, but I've tortured myself by imagining how she was murdered. I could have done so much more for her: brought her home to meet my family, advised her better or found a counsellor for her or something… anything other than leaving her to get on with it. I can't tell you how guilty I feel about that. And now I know you're going to tell me how and where it happened. This is too horrible for words.'

I let the tears run down my face and Lidia, who'd been holding my shoulder since helping me into the chair, took her hand away and let it join the other on her lap.

'OK. Can I ask you again? When were you last in Beaconsfield?'

I looked at Lidia for help, but she looked at her hands.

'It was about four years ago I think. I had a client who recommended me to a person in the old town. I can look at my records if you like,' I said pushing down on the arm of the chair to get up.

'That won't be necessary,' said Cummings.

'Now tell me how she was murdered,' I said.

'I'm going to leave that for now,' said Cummings.

'However, Travner said you were there on the day you told us you were in Regent's Park,' said Edwards.

'That's ridiculous,' I replied.

'You say you don't know Travner and you were not in Beaconsfield on Sunday the ninth of November last year,' stated Cummings.

'That's correct.'

'We've finished. I'm sorry this has been so upsetting for you,' said Cummings, as she rose from the sofa.

'Thank you for your time,' said Edwards.

TWENTY THREE

I've said before that official envelopes jar with me. However, this one looked innocuous enough and the man was cheerful while I signed for it, but my heart rate increased and my tinnitus changed to a very high pitch the moment I read the word "Subpoena".

'From what Cummings said, it looks as though they've accused someone.'

'Why subpoena me then?' I asked Lidia, knowing the question was rhetorical.

'I've no idea. Phone Cummings.'

I was so anxious I couldn't eat breakfast until Cummings returned my call.

'Try not to let it worry you, Mister Johnson. You've told us all you know. Simply repeat it to the court if you're called.'

'Why do I need to go to court at all?'

'We have prosecuted Jack Travner as a result of all our enquiries, but that doesn't stop the defence from introducing anything that may possibly lessen the case against their client. I doubt you will be called. If you are, tell the court what you've told us, no more, no less.'

'Thanks for your time, Sergeant. I feel much better.'

I hadn't realised how tense I'd been until I put the phone down. I felt and heard myself breathe out, and I tilted forward as my stomach muscles relaxed.

'Happier?' asked Lidia throwing the word in my direction without looking at me.

I knew she was irritated by my reluctance to take my medication, but I knew it would make me less alert, and I felt I needed my wits about me, in spite of having my emotions continuously close to the surface. I switched off five minutes later when she ranted on about it. I told myself that her diminishing lack of compassion was making me stronger and less dependent on her. We finished our breakfast and cleared up the kitchen in near silence.

I went upstairs to my office, looked at the pinboard, drew comfort from the words "You are innocent" and went through everything I could remember of that Sunday. Clarity eluded me, so I wrote it down. It took me ages, and when I reread it, I added a bit here and there. I reread it again and did the same thing, apart from crossing out something I wasn't certain about, because I got that Sunday confused with the Sunday Lidia and I had gone over the route. By the time I'd finished, my hand was shaking. I stopped and breathed deeply. I later proposed the idea to Lidia of me getting legal help.

'Now you're going overboard.'

I didn't mind her words, but did she really need to roll her eyes skywards as she spoke? Nevertheless, I agreed and felt belittled, having proposed it.

TWENTY FOUR

I felt Frances's presence, and her unconcerned reaction to the loud clicking of her high heels on the marble floor of the crown court, long before I saw her. Never intimidated, she brought the low, autumn morning sun into the building.

'I'm not a child,' I said.

'I don't care. Mum told me you didn't want a witness volunteer, so you've got me instead. I'm staying here until you're called. Mum will join you back here after you've finished giving evidence, as I have to go back to my office.'

Contrary to what I'd said to Frances earlier, I welcomed her support, and the two hours we waited for me to be called whizzed by in conversation unrelated to the case, which relaxed me considerably.

'Sorry to have kept you waiting,' said the court usher. 'The court is now ready for you.'

Frances and I stood up. She turned to me and gave me a hug.

'You look great, Dad.'

I looked about the courtroom not daring to search out Lidia and was surprised at people's apparent indifference to my entry. Only the judge looked directly at me. The other official-looking people were either concentrating on their papers, or talking in hushed voices. When I'd completed the "Witness Affirmation" for which I'd elected in place of an "oath", the court became silent and a stocky, red-faced man in a wig seemed to want to prolong the silence by rising slowly and adjusting his spectacles.

'Mr. Johnson, could you please tell the court how you spent the afternoon of Sunday the 9th of November 2003.'

His eyes turned from me to the jury as though illustrating where "the court" was.

I slowly and deliberately described every physical and emotional aspect of that Sunday as if telling Lidia for the first time. It simplified my response. I managed to block out the court, and it felt strangely cathartic.

'What was your reaction when Miss Wadzinski, Zuzanna, failed to turn up?' asked my inquisitor.

I explained that I felt a load had been lifted from me and that I'd consoled myself in the belief that she'd solved her problems, or that she couldn't get away.

'Either way,' I said, 'I knew I didn't want to see her again.'

'Did you expect to hear from her again?'

'Yes. I thought she'd phone to say why she hadn't turned up.'

'What would you have done?'

'I'd resolved to tell her that I would not be meeting her again regardless of her reason.'

'Why was that?'

'I'd helped her as much as I could, and I didn't want to become involved.'

'Did you ever speak to her again after that?'

'No.'

My questioner thanked me and sat down. Another equally stocky and red-faced man, with what appeared to be an ill-fitting wig, got up. He turned slightly towards the jury and smiled.

'I put it to you, Mr. Johnson,' he said loudly, 'that you, as you said in so many words, had had enough of Miss Wadzinski because she was a threat to your family life and you decided to get rid of her.'

'That's not true.'

'What's not true? That she was a threat to your family or that you had had enough of her?'

The man who questioned me first started to stand but, before he could say anything, the judge said, 'I agree, Mr. Neville.' The man then sat down.

'Did you decide to get rid of her?'

I just looked at my accuser.

'Please answer the question, Mr. Johnson,' said the judge.

'Of course I didn't.'

'We'll take that as a "no". However,' he continued, looking away from me and directly at the jury, 'you did know Mr. Travner.'

Neville quickly rose but, before he could say anything, my accuser turned back to me and said, 'Did you know Mr. Travner, Mr. Johnson?'

'No.'

'He knows you, Mr. Johnson. Furthermore, he has described how you and he disposed of Miss Wadzinski's body after *you* killed her.'

I looked at a mole above the man's lips. I watched his wig perched very slightly to one side and thought, *How careless – you couldn't paint a straight line if you tried.* I saw the colours of items around the court. I saw the jury for the first time as individuals. I wasn't afraid to look up at the visitors. I saw Lidia and others and pondered about their choice of clothes for the event and their interest in the case. I felt alive and confident, in the face of this pompous man, as though welcoming a challenge or even a fight. I was so very pleased that I'd not taken my medication. I watched my accuser's eyes focused somewhere between the jury and me.

'Have you nothing to say about that, Mr. Johnson?'

'I'll answer you honestly when you've asked me a question,' I replied.

One of the visitors quickly stifled a laugh. Then I saw everyone for the performing artists that they really were.

'Did you kill Miss Wadzinski, Mr. Johnson?'

'I did not harm Zuzanna Wadzinski in any way whatsoever,' I replied. 'So the answer is no.'

I was going to elaborate but remembered Frances's words, 'say as little as possible'.

'I put it to you, Mr. Johnson, that you met Mr. Travner soon after leaving your house. You were then driven in his car to pick up Miss Wadzinski at the flat she shared with her boyfriend, knowing he was out for the day. The three of you went to a lonely track near Beaconsfield where a sex game got out of hand and, while Mr. Travner was having a cigarette, you killed Miss Wadzinski with blows to her head with a crowbar. Having done your dirty deed, you set fire to the car and made your way to Beaconsfield, where you caught a train back to London.'

'That's ridiculous.'

'Is it? You don't have anything to substantiate your whereabouts on the day in question because you weren't where you said you were, were you, Mr. Johnson?'

'I've told you exactly where I was.'

My accuser raised his shoulders while looking at the jury, turned to the judge and said he had no more questions.

Drained and shocked by the experience, I left the court and waited for Lidia. She arrived a few minutes later with Constable Edwards.

'Sorry you had to go through that,' said Edwards. 'We hoped Travner would plead guilty to try and get a more lenient sentence and you wouldn't be needed.'

'Who is this Travner? What's his bloody motive?' asked Lidia.

'I can't...' but before Edwards could finish, Lidia broke in.

'Did you know that disgusting man was going to accuse Frank of murder?'

'We didn't think...' but again Lidia interrupted.

'Point-scoring little runt. Couldn't even look Frank in the eye.'

'He's only doi...' I started to say.

'He has no idea of the damage he's done. No bloody idea whatsoever. I've a good mind to wait for him to come out and confront the conniving bastard.'

Lidia sat down on the bench and searched through her bag, while Edwards and I sat either side of her.

'Does Travner work for Jordache?' I asked.

'I can't say,' replied Edwards. 'What I can say is that, unless he brings a big rabbit out of the hat, he'll be put away for a long time.'

An usher came to us from the courtroom.

'You will not be required further, Mr. Johnson. You may go.'

'Thank God for that!' said Lidia. 'I've had enough. Our family's been pulled apart by this whole thing, and I know this will resonate for a long time because of that posing runt in there.'

'I'm sorry you're upset,' said Edwards.

'You and Cummings are not blameless either,' she said accusingly, getting up and making for the door. She didn't see me shake hands with Edwards.

'Do you want a cup of tea?' I shouted to Lidia, as she removed her coat in the hallway.

'Pour me a red wine!' she shouted back.

I choked back a comment about wine at four in the afternoon.

We sat in the lounge cradling our thoughts in silence, Lidia with her red wine and me with a cup of tea. I would have enjoyed a glass of wine, but I felt I needed to think clearly and absorb everything that had happened. Fifteen minutes later, I'd compartmentalised my thoughts and needed to be active, or at least plan to be active.

'We have the whole weekend,' I said. 'What would you like to do?'

'It's not over yet, and there's no way I can flit about pretending it is,' she replied spitting the words out as if they tasted foul.

'You heard Edwards. He said...'

'That bitch, Cummings, said you were going to court to state your whereabouts and that would be that. Then that horrid man transferred his imagination to the jury, and the bastard looked as though he had them. Half the bloody jury looked willing to go down any avenue he'd lead them. The whole fucking thing was a farce.'

For a second or two I hoped Lidia would burst into tears. I wasn't prepared to make myself vulnerable to her raw anger by touching her.

'Come on, Lidia, cross-examination was always on the cards,' I said, but she wasn't listening as she retrieved the ringing phone from the hall.

'I'll have another wine,' she said handing me the empty glass and the phone as though they were contaminated.

'How are you, Dad? Mum said you were ambushed by some nasty little runt.'

'I'm OK-ish,' I replied.

'That doesn't sound good.'

'I was quite shaken by him, but that's his job.' As I said this, I thought of George Carmen QC acting for *The Sun* newspaper and reducing Gillian Taylforth to an unconscious wreck.

'I'm coming over,' said Frances.

'No, leave it. It'll only upset your mum, and I don't want to relive the event.'

After a minute or so, while still talking to Frances, Lidia snatched the glass off the telephone table and muttered something about filling her own bloody glass.

'You still there, Dad?'

'Yes. Sorry. I was supposed to be getting a glass of wine for your mother.'

'Concentrate on looking after yourself, Dad. Mum's so pissed off she can't think of anything else. She'll come round. Don't get anxious and don't force her into a conversation.'

I put the phone down feeling somewhat better, and thought of Frances as a four-year-old and wondered what experiences had made her so wise and, not for the first time, a shiver went through me as I thought how close she was to not being born at all.

Lidia and I went upstairs after the ten o'clock news. I sat on the edge of the bed and watched her slip out of her plain cotton pants without a trace of emotion. Lace and silk had disappeared leaving further evidence of utility. *All caused by me*, I thought.

I couldn't sleep while mentally listing my guilt and, by the time I got out of bed two hours later, I'd reached an intolerable pitch of self-loathing. I went to my office with a cup of tea, intending to write everything down, in the hope of resolving our situation. I cried without shame while writing, and became too distraught to go back to bed once I considered the possibility of the case against Travner collapsing, and the police reinvestigating me.

Frances phoned the following day.

'It'll soon be over, Dad.'

'I'm glad, but what if they find him not guilty?'

'That's their problem.'

'It could be mine. I don't have an alibi for that day, and the police could interrogate me again.

'No… not at this stage, Dad,' she said with less conviction than I'd hoped.

'And what if he's not guilty and the jury find him guilty?'

'Stop it, Dad, for God's sake!'

TWENTY FIVE

The next night, I thought my head was on fire. I was clammy with sweat when I awoke at two thirty after hearing my accuser's voice.

'I put it to you, Mr. Johnson, that you killed Miss Wadzinski.'

I could see the jury, as it had been that day, nodding in agreement and the judge, who'd taken his wig off, had allowed his long hair (or was it Zuzanna's?) to fall over his shoulders and cover the front of his gown. He was smiling and congratulating my accuser while they looked at me.

'I really think you should take those tablets,' said Lidia. 'You're not getting any sleep.'

'Sorry, I didn't mean to wake you.'

'I've been awake for ages with your fidgeting.'

'Sorry,' I repeated.

I carefully got out of bed and went to Frances's old room and made the bed up.

I felt I'd been asleep for a long time when I heard someone saying, 'I don't... I don't... I don't...'

It took a few seconds to realise it was me, but I couldn't

recollect the scene of my dream. I held my wristwatch close to my face and could just make out the phosphorescent glow of 04:50. I got out of bed and went to my office where I reflected on that Sunday, convinced I'd drawn cash from a machine. *If I got that wrong, what else did I get wrong?* I thought.

Unstable, fragile, unhinged, call it what you like, or even mad, come to that. I felt I was on the edge of a precipice. Deep down, I expected to feel like that, almost inviting it, instead of being happy when I was told by the police that they were confident of convicting Travner. Deeper still, I'd become obsessed with my guilt about the damage I'd done to Lidia and my family which, in my state of mind, eclipsed anything the court had to offer.

I reflected on a time when the girls freely chatted with Lidia and me over dinner. Now I could no longer speak from a moral high ground, imagined or real. They also saw, not only my weakness as someone who strayed from the path that kept the foundation of their home intact, but as someone diminished by that action and now cowed. They could see the toll on Lidia, no longer the lively, imaginative contributor to their conversations. She'd adopted a mantle of seriousness which aged her, and her happy shopping sprees with the girls no longer happened. *Had I been a burden over the years? Had I undermined our relationship so much that she felt insecure? Had she lost her sense of fun forever? Was she getting at me?* For a brief moment, I thought I saw some resolution within my despair and the debris of our reduced lives, but I recalled the short shrift I received when I suggested we see a counsellor together. I think she'd heard enough about the occasional voices in my head, witnessed my extreme lows and didn't know how to avoid them. She'd also almost given up suggesting I took my medication.

I felt myself slipping into a depth of despair I'd not been in before, and I had illusions of imagined relief at the thought of being found guilty, as though it would absolve me from all my accumulated guilt since being a child and would rid me of all mental torture. I remember sitting in my office, going through whatever reasoning I had left, in the hope of finding a way out but, in my anguished state, I could only think of the River Thames as an invitation to an end.

I then heard Becky's anxious voice getting louder and felt my arm being pushed back and forth.

'Are you alright, Dad?'

I opened my eyes, saw Becky's knees near my face and the underside of my office desk, without immediately knowing what it was.

'I'm fine,' I replied, as I gathered my senses together.

'What are you doing on the floor?'

'I needed to lie on a flat surface after working early this morning, and I must have fallen asleep.'

'See you downstairs.'

I brushed my teeth, dressed and joined the others in the kitchen where each of them seemed to be in their own world in preparation for the day. Minutes later, after a coffee and toast, everyone dispersed in a cacophony of conversation aimed at nobody in particular, and I was alone to finish clearing up.

TWENTY SIX

I'd excelled in the quality of my work until my performance in court. In fact, I know now that my functioning had relied solely on my work to the exclusion of everything else. Only afterwards, when I stood back and looked at Lidia and the girls, did I understand that my self-support had been leading me to the edge of an abyss.

The wake-up call came when, five days after being in court, an apologetic client phoned to say he was getting another contractor to finish one of my jobs. I remember it well. It was the same day I grazed the van on the wall to our drive.

I didn't work the following day.

'I'll phone Mr. Herrington,' said Lidia looking at my work schedule, 'and you go back to bed. I'll phone the doctor.'

'I don't need a bloody doctor.'

Lidia stood back. I noticed her eyes becoming watery, a tear breaking loose from one eye and it following the side of her nose.

'Please...' she started to say before turning to leave the room.

I smashed my fist down on the keyboard, breaking it, as

she closed the door behind her. I tore it from the computer and threw it in the bin, knocking it over. The only thing I remember after that was pulling the duvet over me.

'How long have you been there?' I asked Frances while struggling to sit up.

'Not long.'

'What time is it?'

'Three in the afternoon.'

'Shouldn't you be at work?'

'Not under the circumstances, Dad.'

I searched her serious face for clues.

'I don't think you're well, Dad.'

'Have you taken time off to be here?'

'Yes.'

'Well, you shouldn't have. Let me be. I'll be OK.'

'I could say, who's been sleeping in my bed, but I won't. What are you going to do, Dad?'

I swung my legs off the bed and sat with my head in my hands.

'I don't know. The more I think about that Sunday when that young woman was killed, the more uncertain I am about myself. It's driving me crazy, because I can't think about anything else. You didn't see that man in court accusing me of murder. He described everything in such detail that I could see it and feel it. I still do. And all I can hear, when I try and sleep, is his voice telling me I did it and asking me for proof of where I was. And I can't bloody well do it,' I shouted. 'Every night… the same bloody thing. And sometimes during the day.

'OK, Dad, OK. But you know the police have got their

man,' she said.

'Got *a* man,' I shouted to her disappearing back.

I knew she was reporting back to Lidia, but I could only hear a few words that flowed towards me as I stood at the top of the stairs.

'Clinging on… wittering… cash… can't force him… see someone… has tablets… course he's innocent… can't… lost it… can't see it… ATMs…'

I heard more as I crept down the stairs while Lidia's voice grew louder.

'Those cops led him into it… knew it… cross-question… drive anybody mad… had it… alibi obsession… Enough, I can't take it!'

I couldn't face entering the room, and when I heard Lidia crying, I crept back upstairs. I spent the next ten minutes, in the shower, vigorously scrubbing every part of me in the hope of ridding myself of me before the hubbub of the girls coming home and the preparation of dinner got under way.

Freshly shaven and holding myself tall, I walked into the kitchen to help as usual and pretended to be unaware of what I had heard earlier. Lidia accepted my kiss on her cheek with the resignation of someone who had seen false starts before. Frances studied the scene as a person might watch a play with the intention of reviewing it later.

Lidia looked at her watch. 'Frances is staying over and the girls will be here in fifteen minutes.'

'What can I do?'

'We're OK. I suggest you make up Frances's bed with fresh linen and get your office sorted out.'

It took me a second or two to register.

'Ah, yes.'

I enjoyed making Frances's room shipshape, subconsciously attracting her to stay more frequently, I suspect. I then opened the door of my office to self-imposed humiliation and got down to the task of assessing the damage and tidying it up. Frances soon joined me.

'I've been thinking about what you said about the ATMs on that Sunday. Did you contact the bank?'

'I've kept all my records, and there were no transactions on that day.'

'Oh! What a pity. By the way, Mum said dinner's ready.'

I felt sheepish when I joined them for dinner and was grateful for Frances's chatter drawing attention away from me.

TWENTY SEVEN

My head touched the pillow, my eyes closed and there he was. Not as he'd been in court, but much taller, more conspiratorial, his wig was straight and he looked less jowly. I expected him to say, 'I put it to you…' Instead, he quietly asked me why I did it. I felt the familiarity of a room without being able to place it. I think it was our lounge, but I couldn't swear to it. Lidia was somewhere near, but each time I looked for her, she seemed to move out of my line of vision. I was sure there were one or two others there. I didn't feel anxious, in fact I felt supported, as though they were easing something out of me like a parasitic worm being gently pulled from my flesh in the hope of not breaking it.

'Tell me why?' he asked.

'I wanted her out of my life for ever.'

'You'll feel much better now,' he said, as I lay back on a couch I didn't recognise and turned over.

I turned over, opened my eyes and lay rigid, convinced there were people in the room. The bed was click, click, clicking to the rhythm of my heart and the dim, reflected light from Lidia's open eyes startled me. She touched my arm.

'Did I wake you?' I whispered.

'I haven't been to sleep.'

'I'm sorry.'

'You were talking.'

'What did I say?'

'Nothing that made any sense, just the odd word.'

'I've slept well. Can I get you anything?'

'No thanks, we've only been in bed ten minutes!'

The dream became etched into my psyche and calmed me. The next thing I knew, it was 07:45 and I heard the familiar sound of the family. Wanting to say cheerio to Becky and Emma, I changed and washed in record time.

'The pair of you have hardly said a word,' I said to Lidia and Frances, as the front door closed on the girls.

'Are you...?' they said in unison.

'I'm fine. Sorry about yesterday. What are you two doing today?'

'I'm working from home,' replied Lidia.

'And I'm going to have a real lazy day and probably get under Mum's feet. And tomorrow is Saturday, and I'm going into town from here, so you've got me for another night.'

I started clearing the breakfast things away.

'I'll make a couple of calls and probably be away by ten for the rest of the day,' I said getting up to clear the table.

I went to my office and sat in my chair looking for inspiration to start work, but I kept reflecting on my dream and reclaiming the calm it gave me. However, it rendered me impotent and unable to plan. My neat files, my well-organised office, my list on the pinboard, my very being, all felt pointless as though there was no future. I didn't feel depressed. I felt nothing. I may even have been asleep when I heard a knock on the door.

Frances placed a letter on my desk.

'Here, Dad. I've written a letter to your bank for you to sign. I'll post it immediately.'

I read it with little interest, signed it and handed it back.

'I spoke to the bank a long time back and they sent me a fresh statement, but if you want to confirm it, then send it.'

Frances left without a word, but her intervention initiated a thread of thinking that disturbed me sufficiently to examine my perception of the world. I suddenly felt cold and frightened and decided to phone Cummings.

TWENTY EIGHT

'Please may I come to the station? I'd like to talk about the case.'

'The case is still being heard, Mr. Johnson,' said Cummings. 'You've helped us with our enquiries, and we've seen no reason for an official statement from you. Have you anything to add?'

'No, but I'd like to talk about the case.'

'We are not able to answer questions about the case.'

I inadvertently raised my voice. 'I just want to talk about something, that's all, and I don't want to talk over the phone.'

'Hang on a moment. If you get cut off, phone back.'

I was about to put the receiver down, after two minutes of silence, when I heard her curt voice.

'Four o'clock with Constable Edwards, is that OK?'

'Yes, thank you.'

'How do you know you have the right man in Travner?' I asked Edwards.

Edwards frowned and asked if I had any further information.

'No.'

'Why are you asking about Travner?'

'The more I think of what I said I did on that Sunday, the more unreal it seems.'

Edwards' frown deepened while he studied the tabletop. After a few seconds of silence, he got up from his seat, walked towards the door and glanced at me.

'Excuse me… I'll be back in a moment.'

He returned a few minutes later with a big man who had an air of confidence that radiated from a sun-browned face and a head of thick, white hair. A man who looked fit for someone who appeared to have passed retirement age.

'This is Constable Symonds. I hope you don't mind if he joins us.'

'Afternoon, Mr. Johnson,' said Symonds in a low-pitched, gentle voice, which contrasted sharply with his tough physique. 'No, don't get up,' he said while shaking my hand and smiling broadly.

They both sat down opposite me across the table.

'Do you want to add something to what you've already told us?' asked Edwards.

I suddenly felt very silly and stood up.

'I can't think of anything. That's the problem.'

'Please sit down,' said Edwards.

'Would you like some tea or coffee?' asked Symonds.

'No thanks,' I replied sitting down.

'Have you anything on your mind you'd like to talk about?' asked Symonds.

'I could have saved him,' I said.

'Him?' said Edwards.

I glanced at Symonds and back to Edwards.

'Did I say him?'

'You did,' replied Symonds.

I froze for a split second, as the voice of a long-ago counsellor entered my head: 'You were not responsible. You were a baby at the time.'

'Sorry about that.'

'How? How could you have saved Zuzanna?' asked Edwards.

I quickly went through my pockets for a pack of tissues, as I felt tears fill my eyes. Symonds raised his eyebrows a little while his face retained the smile he had when he entered the room. Edwards' frown returned.

'I should have been firmer with her when we first met. Or even got hold of social services on her behalf. Or insisted she come back to my house and meet my family. Or... I don't know any more.'

Symonds and Edwards were silent, while I pulled myself together.

'I'm being pathetic. I'm sorry.'

'You wanted to know if we had the correct man in Travner. Yes?' asked Symonds.

'Yes.'

'Why does that concern you?'

'I couldn't bear it if there was any doubt,' I replied.

'Can you explain that?'

'Because I'm guilty,' I blurted out.

I was unaware of the time when Lidia rang.

'It's six o'clock and you left without a word. Where are you?'

'I'm at the police station.'

There was a long pause before she asked if the police had

asked me to go there.

'No. I can't talk now. I'll tell you about it when I get home.'

'What time?'

'I'm not sure.'

Lidia put the phone down.

Once I started talking to Symonds and Edwards, I couldn't stop. Everything I felt guilty about came pouring out: Zuzanna's death, my feelings about the disruption I caused my family, my weaknesses leading to my breakdown and then I tried, as I had many times, to grasp an elusive cause of my mental state.

'Earlier you said "him" instead of "her", said Symonds. 'Is there something in that error?'

I stared at Symonds' pleasant, old and powerful face and felt like a child. I wanted to reach out and hug him. More than that, I wanted him to reach out and hug me. I turned away from the table and cried using one tissue after another. Only when I felt composed did I turn back and, for some reason I couldn't fathom, I was not anxious about using their time or about my behaviour.

Then Symonds, in a calm voice said, 'You're telling us you killed Zuzanna because you could have saved her and didn't.'

'Put that way, it sounds illogical,' I replied. 'But I can't bear it any longer.'

'Let us sit quietly for a moment or two,' said Symonds.

'Would you like us to fetch your wife?' asked Edwards.

'No,' I replied.

I wanted to carry on talking. I felt the floodgates to

my mind were open, and the last thing I wanted was any contradiction that could interfere with the flow.

Edwards asked if I'd come by car.

'My van.'

'I think it would be better if you didn't drive,' said Symonds.

'It's my work van, with my work equipment.'

'If you're worried about leaving it here,' said Edwards, 'we can make arrangements to get it home for you.'

'Would you like to tell us more?' asked Symonds.

I put both my hands flat on the table, sat up straight and looked at them both.

'No. That's all. Thank you.'

I looked at the surface of the table and thought of the time Edwards and Cummings witnessed me on the floor of my lounge. I remembered the noise of the train and the scream of a child. I winced and my right knee jumped.

Symonds' eyebrows lifted, inviting further words from me.

'Nothing more?'

'Er, no. I don't think so.'

'I'm not qualified to dig deeper into your understanding of the world, Mr. Johnson, but I recommend you discuss what you've told us with someone better qualified than me.'

I was about to talk about my past therapy and the medication I was supposed to take, but I glimpsed how inappropriate it was.

'I'll do that,' I said.

I got out of my van and thanked the policeman who had driven me home before he walked to the police car that had followed us. The lounge door was shut, which was unusual. I went through to the kitchen and joined Becky and Emma, who were finishing their dinner.

'Mum wanted to talk to Frances,' said Becky.

'Without us,' added Emma looking dejected.

'I'll join them.'

The unusual sound of Frances arguing with Lidia caused me to hesitate.

'I don't know who I'm married to any more,' I heard Lidia say.

'I'm sorry, Mum, but you can't assume anything. I don't want to hear any more.'

I remained riveted to the spot outside the door.

'You heard a few words and you're building your own nightmare. Dad's not well, but he's getting better. You saw him this morning. Now for goodness' sake stop it.'

'It wasn't a few, random words, it was a whole bloody sentence.'

'But you just said you couldn't hear properly, and now you're saying it was as clear as crystal.'

'I didn't say it was as clear as crystal. I said I heard whole sentences.'

'Don't you understand, Mum? He was dreaming.'

'OK, perhaps I'm making mountains out of molehills, but it gave me a shock.'

I heard a chair move, and I quickly took the stairs two at a time to my office before noisily closing the door and walking back down. It would have been easier to catch a fly with one hand than to catch Lidia's eye as she came out of the lounge.

'Well? Did you get what you wanted from the police

station?'

I gave her a peck on the cheek as she spoke.

'Well? Did you?'

'I wanted to know how certain they were about Travner's conviction.'

'And? Did they tell you?'

'Not exactly.'

'What's that supposed to mean?'

'I felt a lot better after I had spoken with them. That's all.'

'What did you talk about?'

'I spoke about my feelings of guilt about everything that's happened. I had to get it off my chest to someone outside the family. That's all.'

Lidia turned away and walked towards the kitchen. 'Dinner's been ready for the last hour.'

Frances joined me in the hallway before I could follow Lidia.

'Hi, Dad. How did it go?'

'Far, far better than I expected. But there again, I don't know what I expected. I phoned on an impulse, and I'm glad I went.'

Frances studied my face.

'You look happier.'

Talk around the kitchen and later during dinner, although stilted, had enough substance, other than my visit to the police station, to keep it pleasantly moving. Later, when Lidia and I were getting ready for bed, I told her about Symonds and my good feelings about him.

'So long as *you're* satisfied, that's what counts.'

I chose to ignore the tinge of sarcasm.

After kissing her goodnight, she turned away, knowing

that neither of us would doze off easily. I woke up at about three o'clock to go to the toilet and couldn't go back to sleep when I returned.

Does she really think I'm implicated in murder? Surely not, I thought. *Do I really have to prove my innocence to my wife?* I knew the strain of putting up with me over the years must have been hard for her. I'd even warned her of my mental fragility before we were married. I often wondered if that was the reason she left me for someone else in our early relationship.

I lay awake gathering the snippets of the conversation I'd heard earlier. I simplified them, amplified them, mixed them up and examined them from a multitude of different views and was no closer to a solution by the first signs of light.

I gave her a mug of tea in bed and sat on the edge of the bed, clutching and sipping mine, while we waited for the new day to truly penetrate our consciousness.

'I'd like to go to a counsellor again and...'

'You go if you want to. I won't.'

'I was hoping we could go together.'

'I could see that coming a mile away. You go. I've had enough psychological games over the years to last me a lifetime.'

She downed her tea and got out of bed.

I had the distinct feeling she was sick and tired of it all and was making plans of her own.

TWENTY NINE

'Morning, Ibrahim.'

Ibrahim looked up from reading the local newspaper, which lay flat on the counter of his small shop.

'Morning, Frank. I bet you're glad that's all over.'

He turned the page back and pointed at "*Murderer and Liar*" in bold print above a man's face on the front page. I'd not told anyone outside the family about the murder case. My smile froze, my mouth dried and the "ding" of the shop's doorbell exploded in my head. Ibrahim's eyes looked up and the corners of his mouth drooped, as he realised the new customer had stolen any conversation with me. He swept the money I'd paid him for *The Guardian* and the local from the counter to his other hand and dropped it into the open till.

'I guessed it was the Frank Johnson that I know. You've not been yourself lately. Have a good day, Frank. Chat tomorrow, eh?'

'Bye, Ibrahim, see you tomorrow.'

'I thought you'd gone to work,' said Lidia.

'It's in the paper.'

I pushed plates and mugs aside and opened the

newspaper on the kitchen counter for us both to read.

"*Murderer and Liar*" the headline read. There was a large, full-face picture of Jack Travner. Below, in small print, was "*GUILTY: Jack Travner, above, faces life in prison for killing Zuzanna Wadzinski, left.*" On the left was a small picture of Zuzanna with the words "*turn to Page 2*". Below was "*Jack Travner killed his friend's girlfriend, set fire to her body, then blamed another man. Yesterday a jury saw through his evil lies*".

My hand shook, as I eagerly turned the page. My mind was already refuting whatever was said about me. Lidia gently cupped my shoulder. I then thought the picture of a man in football gear was unrelated to the rest of the article until I read:

Jordache Essono's girlfriend killed by his long-term friend.

The jury took two hours and 40 minutes to find Jack Travner guilty of battering his friend's girlfriend to death with a crowbar and leaving her body in a burning car.

Travner, 32, was convicted of killing Zuzanna Wadzinski, 30, after an eight-day trial at the Crown Court.

Ms Wadzinski's body was found in a burned-out car near Beaconsfield in November last year.

Travner, of Southwark, London, began a life sentence yesterday, but the minimum length of time he must serve before he can be considered for release was due to be announced by the Judge today.

The court heard how Jack Travner, a long-term friend and associate of Jordache Essono, took Zuzanna Wadzinski to Beaconsfield to look at a house that Jordache Essono was thinking of buying. Travner had become besotted with

Wadzinski and had brutally killed her when she resisted his advances and threatened to tell Essono. Travner had spied on Wadzinski and a friend of hers, Mr Frank Johnson, when they met at a café, and had tried to implicate him.

When it was put to Travner that he was eaten up with jealousy about Johnson's relationship with Wadzinski and wanted Johnson to take the blame for her death, Travner did not reply.

'Happy?' said Lidia, as she walked towards the stairs.

THIRTY

'I don't know any more,' I replied to Frances when she asked me how I felt, now that Travner had been convicted of Zuzanna's murder.

'I have to stop thinking about everything that happened and concentrate on my work. It's recovering well, now that I'm doing six days a week. And besides, it keeps me out of mischief.'

'Are you telling me that the quality of our lives hinges on you working to the exclusion of everything else?'

'You're trying to simplify things, Frances. It's not that easy. It'll take time to come right, and I still can't prove where I was.'

'Do you need to? You know where you were.'

'Please. I don't want to go over that again, because it brings up my doubts about everything.'

She left without smiling.

I carried on being satisfied with my work. When I couldn't get on with any of the decorating jobs, I'd search for imperfections in my accounts, in my planning and even the arrangement of materials and the cleanliness of the van. Finding something tangible was always a relief. Lidia had found excuses to work beyond her three-day agreement and often brought work home. Emma and Becky hardly noticed, or if they did, they didn't say anything. Frances was the only one who challenged us.

'You do realise this is ridiculous,' she said when she and I were alone in my office. 'I want to know what you're going to do to get back to where we all were before this whole thing happened.'

'Nothing, the business is doing extremely well, and I've got so much work ahead of me that I'm vetting the workmanship of some contractors to work with me. In fact, I've scheduled nine months ahead and, do you remember Professor Norris who lives...'

Before I could finish, she slammed her hand on to my desk and shouted.

'Stop it, Dad! I've had enough. I want to know what you're going to do?'

'It's not me, it's...'

'I don't give a shit. I want to know what it takes for you to get this family back. Just bloody well tell me.'

'I can't, and I don't want to talk about it.'

'Well I do. And I want Mum back as she was.'

'Then you must speak to your mother.'

'She's frightened of you having another breakdown. You and she can't see that you're working towards it. So there, I've said it. Now what have you got to say?'

'I'm not working towards anything. Perhaps I've really found peace within my work that I didn't know was possible.'

'Bullshit!'

'OK. Bullshit. But there you are.'

'Did you fuck Zuzanna?'

'No. And there's no need to be so crude.'

'Oh, but there is, Dad. If you are so sure about that, then how come you're not sure about all the other things?'

'How would you feel about not being able to account for a day of your life?'

'Is that it, Dad? Is that what it takes? You can account for your day, but you can't prove it to others. Isn't that it? Don't you realise you're almost telling us not to believe you. Isn't it better to say "I feel so shit about myself that I rely on others to justify my existence"?'

'I wish you'd stop using the word "shit".'

'I suppose Professor bloody Norris said you do wonderful work, and that lets you off the hook and then there's no need for you to take responsibility for yourself. Professor Norris has taken it out of your hands until the next Professor bloody Norris shows up. Wake up, Dad, for Christ's sake! Life is so much bigger than this.'

'You've no idea what it feels like to have voices telling you things,' I shouted back. 'That bastard gave such graphic details of Zuzanna's death, they're embedded deep inside me, and I can't separate them from the hurt I've caused your mother.'

'And me? And while you're about it, why not include Becky and Emma and all our friends who no longer come around for laughs? If you want to flagellate yourself then really go for it.'

'I've had enough of this.'

'So have I. Now stand up and give your daughter a hug.'

I did exactly as I was told while ignoring our tears.

THIRTY ONE

I'm Frances. I'm itching to have my say. Dad's story is also mine, and he's not aware of everything that goes on. Nobody ever is.

Some people think I'm unfortunate to have a dad who has mental problems, but I consider it an advantage. Not always a nice experience but a necessary and important one for me to understand people better, almost a privilege. I'm not naïve in thinking it's for everybody. I'm well aware of people who are happy to sail through life without such ups and downs and, of course, there are those who shy away from, or turn against, people who don't conform to their view of "normal". The evidence is all around us, but I'm not going to get on my high horse about that.

I felt like a malfunctioning satellite being left in space while the launch rocket fell back to Earth when my dad, the very person who'd given me enormous confidence to strike out in life, retreated into his work. I wasn't having it. In spite of my many attempts to help Mum get a grip, she seemed to be letting Dad drift off, while she retreated into her own world. I know she was exhausted by the whole experience of Dad's mental issues and his escapade, or whatever that was, with Zuzanna, but I wasn't having that either.

Mum had been curt, to the point of being rude, to me one evening when I suggested, yet again, she and Dad get professional help.

'Leave me be. I'm not going there again. I don't think I've got the emotional strength to carry on my life as well as that.'

I knew I'd been particularly irritating but, like a dog with a bone, I couldn't leave it alone.

'It depends on your priorities.'

'Stop bloody well nagging me.'

'You know Dad's building himself up to another breakdown. He's avoiding all thoughts relating to the murder case because he's unable to separate it from his guilty feelings about his disloyalty to you. You know he's on the edge of a breakdown. You're going to get involved when it happens, that's for bloody sure. We'll all be sucked into it then.'

'Stop torturing me. And as for talking to your dad, I've done enough mollycoddling to last me a lifetime.'

As tangible as sticking a fork in her leg, Mum was hurting herself. Yes, she'd had doubts about trusting Dad after the initial shock of finding she'd been left out when it came to Zuzanna, but when she said he'd probably fucked her, I lost it, saying I didn't give a shit if he had.

'But I know he didn't,' I added immediately.

I'd used every tool in my box and there was nobody I could call on to talk to Mum. I was desperate.

'It's OK for you to have an affair, but not OK for Dad. Is that it?'

I thought she was going to hit me. I hoped she would, anything that could draw the pus out of this festering ulcer was OK as far as I was concerned. Mum turned away and looked into space.

I took her shoulders and turned her towards me.

'Look at me, Mum. I'm the result of your affair with a man you met after you'd been with my dad. My dad, who loves me, is now upstairs hiding in his work while my biological father doesn't give a shit about me. Do you want me to find him and tell him who I am and how your husband, my dad, saved my life? Do you?'

In spite of my shaking, I was tingling with feelings of being in control. I couldn't comfort her, and I didn't want to. I sat watching her for a full two minutes while she and I recovered.

'OK. Tell me what to do.'

'We go upstairs to Dad's office and sit with him.'

'Then what do we do?'

'We just sit with him.'

'He'll think we've gone mad.'

'He can think whatever he likes.'

THIRTY TWO

My mental alarm bells rang when Frances came into my office with Lidia. I thought it was a deputation bringing some dreadful news.

We sat in silence for a long time. Lidia looked at her hands on her lap. Frances, her elbows on the arms of her chair, kept her eyes on her mother's head as though wishing it to be upright, while I gathered invoices together for filing.

'I don't think I've been much help lately, Frank. I'm sorry,' said Lidia without looking at me.

I wanted to hug her but, sensing the delicacy of the moment, I remained still and quiet for a few seconds.

'I'm not sure how to handle this,' I said. 'I'm really sorry about everything. I feel so wretched. I don't know how to get back to how we were.'

I think I sounded impersonal, but it felt precarious for me to cross a crevasse that had been steadily widening over a long time. I reached for Lidia's hand. She took it and grasped it tightly, before letting go and leaving me with Frances.

'What would we do without you, Frances?'

'Behave like kids.'

'What did you say to her?'

'I'll leave that to Mum.'

I felt drained and only went down to the lounge to join Lidia after an hour. I kissed the top of her head, and she reached up with her hand for me to take. We remained like that while watching the *10 O'Clock News*.

The feeling I had when official envelopes came through the post had got worse with the toing and froing over the past month or so and, as always, I expected the worst when I saw the windowed monster among the trade correspondence and advertising debris on the sideboard. It had gone five, too late to do anything about its contents so, rather than open it and worry about the findings overnight, I decided to leave it.

'Was there anything from Lloyds in the post today?' asked Frances over dinner.

'Should there be?' I answered.

'I phoned my contact there, and he said it had been sent yesterday.'

'I've not opened all the mail today.'

Frances was up like a shot and brought the envelope back to the table.

'Come on, Dad, open it.'

'What do you think it is?'

'Just open it.'

'It's from Lloyds TSB,' I said.

'Stop taunting us, Dad, either read it or give it to Mum or me.'

The penny still hadn't dropped while I read aloud.

Please find enclosed details of your ATM withdrawal for £100.00 taken from your above numbered account on Sunday the 9th November 2003.

I can't remember who snatched it from my hand, but I still considered it an academic exercise while watching the tops of their heads opposite me sharing the letter. Lidia turned to the second page and looked through listed transactions, leaving Frances to finish page one.

Lidia and Frances looked up. Frances was smiling to the point of laughing, while Lidia remained expressionless. She put the pages together and passed them back to me.

I skipped through the text eager to grasp the facts.

Please find enclosed details of your ATM withdrawal for £100.00 taken from your above numbered account on Sunday the 9th November 2003.

The actual date of the transaction was Sunday 9th November 2003 and the transaction was actioned at 14.59.58 at Lloyds TSB Bank... Enclosed is the ATM statement that has been sent from our ATM Reciprocity department confirming these details. The transaction was done with your debit card number XXX.

Your statement shows your account being debited on Monday the 10th November 2003 as that is the first working day after the original transaction and a bank statement cannot show a weekend date.

If I can be of any further assistance, please do not hesitate to contact me at this office.

Yours sincerely,

XXXXX XXXXXX
Manager: Customer Services

'She's marked the corresponding bank transaction with a star on the next page, Dad.'

I felt numb as I looked down the columns.

The three of us stood in the kitchen and hugged each other. I felt disoriented when I knew I should have felt elated. I even battled to control my voice.

'I need to be alone for a while to gain some sense of perspective.'

I went to my office and looked at the work schedule chart, the pristine neatness of my paperwork, the coloured lever arch files, each depicting specific content, the matching tiered and labelled filing trays, my computer screen neatly positioned next to the printer on part of the desk, leaving a clear space to read and take notes on the other, my special filing cabinets for trade magazines and documents, my three expensive matching swivel chairs and desk and the perfectly decorated office under well-placed lights. *This is me*, I thought, before reflecting on my new (always clean) van, with its perfectly displayed logo, parked perfectly in the drive. *Am I really this, to the exclusion of everything? My six-day working week and my Sunday to cement my perfection in place?*

I had a shower and went to bed oblivious of Lidia's thoughts and feelings.

THIRTY THREE

Lidia here. I have to come back in to say what I feel and felt.

As I've said, Frank had, and still has, an inner strength, so when he showed his obsessive side, as his affair with Zuzanna started to unravel (I call it an affair, but I don't think he had sex with her and, in some way, I wished he had), I got a bit nervous and gave up making suggestions. I regret refusing to go to a counsellor with him, although by then, I had more on my plate than I could handle.

I thought he'd be over the moon with the letter from the bank, but it seemed to jar with him rather than set him free. I felt relieved at the time on his behalf, with only a tinge of relief for myself, because I knew deep down that Frank was telling the truth. It was only later, when he started to doubt himself, that I needed to stick with his story and not allow myself to follow the warping of his reality. That's probably what exhausted me, now that I think about it.

I sat in the lounge with a glass of red wine and the light off when Frank had gone upstairs and Frances had gone home. I thought about the police not bothering to retrieve the information from the bank, the insensitivity of the prosecution, Frank for getting himself into the situation in the first place and hiding it from me, Frances for taking my role in defending Frank and the whole bloody world for conspiring to disrupt our family.

Of course there was more. Perhaps even my jealousy of Frances and her privileged position of beloved daughter. I'm being sarcastic, but I'm not going back on it. I was raging by the time I went to the kitchen and poured the rest of my wine down the sink. I went to my desk and wrote a long list of injustices.

I was still raging when I phoned Cummings at nine the following morning.

'I have further evidence with regard to the Wadzinski case,' I calmly said to her.

'I appreciate your call, Mrs. Johnson, but as you know, the case is closed.'

'I have important information,' I persisted.

'Please tell me.'

'I can only tell you face to face and preferably while Edwards is present.'

'I'll need to arrange that with Edwards. I'll phone you back, Mrs. Johnson.'

I had the wind behind me as I entered the police station.

'Why did you want to have access to all my husband's bank details if you couldn't see anything deeper than the average person in the street?'

That was my opening gambit to Cummings and Edwards. I know I behaved badly, rather like a banshee at one stage, but the pair of them hardly flinched and allowed me to run out of steam. Afterwards, I handed over a letter I'd prepared which, by then, felt as weak as water compared with my rant.

I walked home feeling justified, satisfied and back on an equal footing with my daughter, Frances. She was home when I got there and confirmed my feeling with 'Good on you, Mum,' after reading a copy of the letter, which I've added at the end of my say here.

Frank seemed deep in thought during our "full house" dinner that evening. He chipped in, in a sort of neutral way, but the buoyancy of the others diluted his input. However, at the end of the meal, when Frank said he was going back to his office to finish a few things, Frances followed him.

Crown Court:
27th September – 8th October 2004
Regina v Travner

I am writing with reference to the above case.

My husband, Frank Johnson, was a witness and received psychological damage by being unnecessarily interrogated. It was hard enough to have sat in court and listened to the dreadful accusations against him because he could not prove his account of his whereabouts on the 9th of November last year. However, I'm not only angry about his treatment by you and the court, I'm now confused as to why it occurred at all.

I enclose a letter from my husband's bank, which came into our hands after the trial. Please read it.

The letter clearly states that Frank withdrew £100 on the 9th November 2003 at 14.59.58 from an ATM along the route he said he'd been on that day and not on Monday 10th of November as his bank statement reflects.

If my daughter could find this information through a Bank Manager Customer Service department, I wondered why the police couldn't have done this back in June, when the accusation came to light. Frank gave his full permission for you to look into any of his personal bank and telephone accounts.

This vital piece of evidence would have saved you wasting your time, our time, and the court's time. Your incompetence inflicted incalculable pain on this family.

I would appreciate a reply on this matter, especially as we were assured that Frank would probably not be needed as a witness.

Yours faithfully,

Lidia Johnson

cc His Honourable Judge xxx.
  Crown Court

THIRTY FOUR

I knew I was in for a grilling the moment Frances got up from the dining table. Sitting in my office on one chair while she took another was like a visit to the dentist. You know it'll hurt, but you also know it's for your own good.

'You still don't know how to return to the family do you, Dad?'

'It'll take time. I can't simply pretend all is behind me and nothing has happened.'

'You haven't got time, Dad. This family's in limbo and needs you back in the driver's seat, otherwise it's going to carry on being dysfunctional. It needs its life back. What are you going to do about it?'

I couldn't look her in the eye, and I couldn't answer her question without reconfirming my recently found comfort within my increased workload, and it wasn't possible to put into words how psychologically precarious I felt outside it. I had started to regard all my past life as a phase that had been good but, a bit like anticipating an old movie for the second time, I felt its appeal had diminished sufficiently to not bother. I couldn't disclose my thinking to Frances and, consequently, I sat patiently waiting for her to go so that I could get on with things.

'That letter from the bank was only a sticking plaster to put over the wound. It won't heal it, Dad.'

'It's complicated.'

'It is. And there's more.'

'How do you mean "more"?'

'More revelations and more work for you to get yourself better. You're not there yet, Dad. Not by a long way.'

'I'm tired.'

'Too tired to get the family back on track, but not too tired to work nine hours a day for six days a week.'

'That's not fair.'

'I don't give a fuck whether it's fair or not.'

Frances always knew she'd get my attention by using expletives. I think she saw it as a challenge. She did it as a teenager to confirm her independence and test the limits of her freedom.

'OK, wise one, what do I do?'

'The business won't suffer. You've got what it takes to handle all that, but you'll need help for the rest.'

'You're proposing counselling, but your mum won't go. You know that.'

'She can do whatever she wants, Dad, but you've got lots on your plate.'

'What's on my plate?' I asked feeling uncomfortable.

'You're the one to find that out, Dad. Find a counsellor you feel you can trust and start soon.'

'How come you know all this?'

'They're your words to me when I had difficulties with relationships. And don't kid me you've forgotten. I also think that's what you told Zuzanna.'

'I don't know that I need to see anybody now. I think it will resolve itself over time from here.'

I sensed she was steeling herself for an onslaught, and I felt I wasn't up to it, but there was no going back without both of us getting hurt.

'I'm guessing, Dad, but from what I've gleaned from everything I've heard, I think Zuzanna loved you, and I think you loved her. No, Dad… please don't try and stop me… and with what's been going on, you've not been able to mourn your loss of her.'

I had a lump in my throat, and I couldn't look Frances in the face. We sat in silence for a while.

'Anything else?'

'The buried anger with the police, the loss of Mum's support while you were emotionally vulnerable, the reasons for your spell in hospital, being unable to forgive yourself for keeping secrets from the family, obsessive behaviour with your work, grasping accolades and approval from outside the family and… and… and… I don't know, Dad, I'm making it up, but there's months of sessions in there.'

'Do you think your mum would come with me?'

'I'm convinced of it. I now know how to persuade her.'

The End

AUTHOR'S NOTE

Some people will admit to a crime they did not commit in order to rid themselves of torment caused by something deep within them that they may not understand. Fortunately, the British legal system continuously evolves to become more just by using tools such as the Gudjonsson Suggestibility Scale (GSS) and police interviewing techniques have evolved in parallel with these.

"There are many different motivations for people making false confessions," says Gisli Gudjonsson, a professor of forensic psychology who helped overturn dozens of wrongful convictions, including the Birmingham Six and Guildford Four.

"The most common is that people can't cope with police interrogation or the pressure of the custody confinement."

"He identified factors in an individual's personality - nothing to do with having a low IQ - that would make them more or less prone to pressure when being questioned. "Other people may just be confusing fantasy and reality," he says, "or they want to be punished for another misdemeanour and it makes them feel better."

Gísli Hannes Guðjónsson, CBE (born 26 October 1947) is an Icelandic-British academic, educator, forensic psychologist and former detective. He is Emeritus Professor at the Institute of Psychiatry of King's College London and a Professor in the Psychology Department at Reykjavik University. Gísli is an internationally renowned authority on suggestibility and false confessions and is one of the world's leading experts on false memory syndrome. (Wikipedia 2022)

The frequency of false confessions is unknown, although a US campaigning group, the Innocence Project, estimates that of 235 convictions overturned due to DNA evidence in the last 15 years, a third involved false confessions.

The two letters within this book are similar to the originals pertaining to a man who felt the need to admit to a murder in England in 2003. Minor changes have been made to accommodate this story and its prime character, Frank Johnson.

ABOUT THE AUTHOR

H E Roffey was born in London. He has worked in the UK, Zambia, South Africa, Europe, America and Australia and now resides in Oxford with his wife, Sonja, a retired lecturer.

His first book "Missed Opportunities" (2018), received excellent reviews. His short story "Loving and Fighting", a story of love, passion and bull fighting in Colombia and the realities of Oxford, was selected for the October 2020 edition of the Oxford Indie Book Fair Magazine. Seven additional short stories were published in 'Tales From An Oxford Café', a compilation of stories from Walton Street Writers, Oxford.

ALSO BY HAROLD ROFFEY

Missed Opportunities

The first in a series of novels exploring the actions of various characters as they face pertinent and moral issues.
From quiet Oxford to drama in the wilds of the Kalahari.

Victor, a law professor with two daughters, muddles along after the death of his wife until he is burgled by Andy.
Cindy, Andy's mother, who has unfulfilled aspirations, gets involved.

Victor and Cindy help each other, but cruel and violent, Andy, and one of Victor's daughters, separately attempt to break up their relationship. A major incident leads Victor to thoughts of murder. Could he carry it out and live with himself, or is he able to find an alternative answer?

Printed in Great Britain
by Amazon

85871395R00082